EMBRACE COURAGE

Finding Strength in the Face of Adversity

EMBRACE COURAGE

Finding Strength in the Face of Adversity

Curated by Cathy Derksen

Action Takers Publishing™
San Diego, California

For bulk orders, reach out to us at www.ActionTakersPublishing.com

ISBN # (paperback) 978-1-956665-20-8

ISBN # (Kindle) 978-1-956665-21-5

Published by Action Takers Publishing™

TABLE OF CONTENTS

Introduction

Far too often when people refer to courage, they are speaking strictly of dramatic displays of courage such as rushing into a burning building to rescue a child. We tend to minimize the courage that is required to get through major challenges and transitions in life. The courage it takes to stand alone and stick to your morals, especially in the face of opposition, requires enormous strength! Protecting our family and setting boundaries to protect ourselves also needs to be acknowledged as courageous.

My intention with this book is to both inspire you to embrace courage in your own life, and to remind you not to minimize the amazing acts of courage you have displayed and witnessed in everyday life.

The members of this wonderful international team of authors have all embraced courage in their own way and have felt compelled to share their journey here with you.

I would like to thank each of them for taking on this challenge. Sharing your stories with the world takes enormous courage.

I am honored to have been entrusted with their work and I am proud to be part of each one's individual journey into growing as an author.

If any of the stories resonate with you, dear reader, please reach out to them. Their contact information is at the end of their chapter.

Cathy Derksen

SPECIAL NOTE: Because of the wide range of authors from all over the world, you may notice that some words are spelled in British English and others in American English. We decided to leave the spellings native to the tongue of the author. Enjoy!

Foreword

"Real courage is being afraid, but doing it anyway"
~Oprah Winfrey

It takes courage to feel and act upon the nudge to bring people together for collaboration. Cathy Derksen has done this and so much more, breathing belief into those of us within this book that our story does matter. By our sharing, others will be elevated and find solidarity, perhaps sensing that they are not alone on this life journey.

The first time Cathy asked me to participate, I did not feel I had much to share in the area of courage. I was also working on my own book and did not want additional distraction. There was a massive hiccup in my writing as my father entered hospice (you, dear reader, will find the story within). My mind went blank and weeks went by without any inspiration to write. At one point, I thought the idea to write a book was foolish and I was ready to abandon my efforts. Then Cathy invited me with gentle encouragement to reconsider contributing a chapter to this book. This time I actually had something to say about courage and was able to write my piece in just a few hours. Cathy saw what I could not see. By priming my writing pump with one chapter, I could return to my own masterpiece with fresh eyes and vision and a desire to write again.

You have a story within you. A story that yearns to be shared. If you find yourself in the presence of one who brings people together to write on a topic that you have lived through and through, say yes to the experience. Your life will be blessed and so will the lives of others.

May these stories be a blessing to you,

Tina Moreau-Jones

Embrace the Courage to Shine

Cathy Derksen

Our deepest fear is not that we are inadequate. Our deepest fear is that we are powerful beyond measure. It is our light, not our darkness, that most frightens us.

Your playing small doesn't serve the world.

As we let our own light shine, we unconsciously give other people permission to do the same.

~Marianne Williamson
Excerpts from A Return to Love

For many years I have felt a calling to step into a bigger, brighter version of myself. I have felt a knowing that I was meant to be a leader in a much bigger way than I had been allowing myself to reveal. Finding the courage to step into this reality has been my journey for many years now. One step forward, two steps back. Owning this new identity, as a leader on an international level, has required me to embrace the courage to shine in a much bigger way than I could have ever imagined.

This book is a concrete example of my growth and progress. I am proud to be the curator of this collaborative book and I am honored to have so many amazing people entrust me with their stories. I am thrilled to step deeper into the roll of international leadership and supporting women and men to share their stories and step into their truth. It may not seem like a large step, but embracing the courage to reach out to people around the world and inviting them to join me on this journey takes a lot of courage. Finding new ways to be brave has helped me tremendously along the way. At the beginning of 2022, I chose 'Courage' to be my focus word for the year.

As I look back over my life, I see so many times when I stepped up into a bigger version of myself, but each time I allowed myself to get caught up into fear and uncertainty. Each time I shrunk back into the smaller version of myself again.

Don't get me wrong. During those times, when I let my light shine, I did accomplish some amazing things. In my early teens, I went from being the kid who sat on the bench eating ice cream during the school sporting events to the kid who was an award-winning athlete in a wide range of sports. At the end of high school, I won a provincial award for all-around athletic, academic, and community achievements. My light was shining bright! I graduated from university with a specialty in Genetics and was chosen as one of only five people to train in a very specialized career in Medical Genetics. That turned into a 25-year career. I like to say, "I've been a biologist since the age of 3." I will always love the field of biology and the magic of life.

As the years went by, I didn't notice my light shifted from burning bright with joy and enthusiasm to dimming to the point of invisibility. A decade ago, I realized that my inner light was almost completely extinguished. It had been a gradual process and when I looked back, I realized that I had been shrinking due to the constant impact of living with an abusive, narcissistic husband at home and a boss at work who needed to keep her staff small in order to protect her own feelings of superiority. While I was in the middle of this situation, I was like the proverbial frog in the boiling water. I had been oblivious to the impact of my circumstances until it was almost too late to rescue my kids and myself from our reality.

Luckily, it hit me like a bolt of lightening which was able to reignite my inner light. This was the beginning of my decade of courage. I left my abusive marriage. I left my toxic boss. I set out on a journey to live life on my own terms. It's been over 12 years now and it has been far from smooth or predictable. Tenacity and courage have become the theme of my life.

This decade of courage has been a journey of rediscovery. I needed to find the version of myself that had been lost along the way due to years of emotional trauma and abuse. As I allowed myself to begin reimagining my life, the fog started to clear in my mind. I learned to trust my intuition again and I gave myself permission to think about a life that would bring back a sense of joy and inspiration to me and my children. They are adults now and I have come to realize how important it is for them to see me stepping into life with courage and enthusiasm.

Throughout this process of personal evolution and growth, I have embraced the courage to take on many huge challenges. Besides leaving my abusive marriage, becoming a single mom, and leaving my toxic job, I also went through two major career changes to get to where I am today.

My mission has been to help women in my community and around the world create a life they love. As I leaned into this vision, I approached it from many angles including providing financial planning services and supporting women through life coaching and mindset transformation. All of these skills and tools were successful in helping women through positive change, but my intuition kept calling me into something bigger. Throughout this process I needed to trust my gut and maintain the courage to keep adjusting and adapting as my path unfolded in front of me.

It's been almost two years since I walked away from my corporate job in financial planning to follow my vision of providing assistance to women that would impact their lives in a powerful, positive way. Through this journey I have come to see that many men are also in alignment with my vision. Stepping out on my own to start my own business and create my own services took far more courage and tenacity than I expected. The learning curve has been steep, and I've had many days when I wondered why I had taken on such a huge challenge. I have named my business Inspired Tenacity. In my view, inspiration and tenacity are two of the key ingredients required to take on any major challenge in our lives. The other key ingredient is courage. Without embracing the courage to follow our vision and stand strong through challenges and opposition, we cannot make big changes in our lives.

My journey as an entrepreneur has been filled with obstacles and points of readjusting and pivoting to find the best way for me to share my gifts and support others. This twisted journey has brought me here, into the world of publishing as the curator of this inspiring collaborative book. A few years ago I would have laughed if you suggested I would become an author and have a career in the publishing industry. At the writing of this chapter, I have seven bestselling books in print with five more in various stages preparing for release. I have found a passion of my own in contributing to these inspiring books and I have come to realize that I have a gift for helping others to clarify their story and to embrace the courage to share it with the world. Being involved in these projects has allowed me to use my inner light to become the lighthouse for so many other people. Sharing our stories is a powerful way to support each other and inspire the reader.

Now I focus my work on creating new collaborative book projects. I create books around themes that inspire both the writer and the reader. I create projects that bring a voice to groups that feel unheard.

After working with the team of authors in this book, I have been so amazed by the range of stories and the depth of wisdom they each bring to the book. The majority of the authors in this book were strangers to me six months ago. Now we have created a bond through this project that will last a lifetime.

I hope my story inspires you to step up and shine your light in a bigger way. If sharing your story in a book feels like your next step, I would love to support you on that journey.

Here is a quote that I have used to inspire myself to keep looking for ways to bring light and life into my work.

"Don't ask what the world needs. Ask yourself what makes you come alive, then go do that! Because, what the world needs is people who have come alive!"
~ Howard Thurman

What makes you come alive? Find it and go do it!

Remember, as Marianne Williamson tells us in the quote that opens my chapter, you are powerful beyond measure and your playing small does not serve the world.

Think big and embrace the courage to step into your dreams. Your brave actions will inspire the people around you to be more courageous in their life as well.

CATHY DERKSEN

Cathy Derksen is the founder of Inspired Tenacity. She is dedicated to improving the lives of the women in her community and around the world. Cathy is an international speaker and a 7x #1 bestselling author with stories that inspire the readers to take a leap of faith into reaching for their big goals. She has created a platform supporting people to share their own inspiring stories in books. With her all-in-one program, Cathy takes you from chapter concept to published bestselling author in a simple, exciting process.

Cathy has two children (28 and 29 years old) and 2 fur-babies. She lives near Vancouver, Canada.

Cathy enjoys spending time in nature, travelling, meeting new people, and connecting with her community around the world.

Learn more about her upcoming book projects and other programs at https://inspiredtenacity.com.

Turning Point

Eric Sharp

This story starts where it ends; late fall in the early '80s around 4:00am, on the eastbound side of a lonely stretch of Yellowhead Highway 16 somewhere between Endako and Vanderhoof in Northern British Columbia. It's not what most would call a highway, just a twisting two-lane ribbon of road that threads through the north country connecting solitary homes, tiny towns, and cities alike, while shrouding lost souls with stories of their own. The road was abandoned at this hour. I'd been pushing my tired but venerable '72 Capri at high speeds for the past hour. The RCMP had all gone home once the bars had closed, and it helped clear my head; concentrate, or die. The car carried everything I owned and was. Once again, I was leaving a place forever. Vancouver was my end destination, where hopefully I'd take up a job that had been lined up many weeks ago. There had been an apartment waiting too, but delays in departure had let that slip away. A rapidly falling fuel gauge had abruptly halted my Exodus at the end of a farmhouse driveway. I had to make a hasty repair on a rusted-out section of fuel line on the frame rail and I lost a half of a tank of fuel. While sitting on a stump at the side of the roadway, waiting for some of the stench of gasoline to dissipate from my clothing, my brain took the time to assay the gravity of my current situation, and try to muster the courage to continue.

That was a lifetime ago. I'm looking back at it now as the man I've become. Since then, there's been time to earn a degree from UC

Berkeley, enjoy a period of marriage, survive a divorce, and return to the Pacific Northwest, having somehow landed in Florida. I'm masquerading as an engineer working in R&D in RV, marine, and portable power products out of my old 1940's home in Portland, OR. My name's on a few patents, and there are a few US airmen that are a lot safer now because of some military contracts I've worked on. But I am sure there is a science fiction writer in there somewhere that is dying to get out. So much water has passed under the bridge since that day on the road, and now the memories seem strange. Like they are not my own.

One of the first memories I have is the day Dad left. Childhood had been blissful up to that point, and Mom kept it that way. She found courage of her own to embrace, as she set about caring for the two of us. I'm sure the good memories from this time kept me sane. It's important to know life can be good at an early age. Then my stepfather entered the picture, and the lines blurred.

I was four years old the first time he displayed a violent outburst over a large fish I had let get away. In this instance he narrowly managed to stay his own hand. The paddle he swung at me whisked through my hair and splintered over the edge of the canoe. He had gone from Jekyll to Hyde in less than a second, but several minutes passed as I watched him put Mr. Hyde back in his box. His dark side wasn't stupid or blind, he knew he couldn't get away with killing a four-year-old with a canoe paddle and that's why I'm still breathing. Stark fear passed through me as I watched him. Then guilt over the broken paddle crept in, and I felt compelled to collect the pieces and try to fix it, as if it was my fault. Why do children feel this way? He motioned for me to be silent, and I suppressed the urge to speak or act. His dark side did not reappear until we moved to a remote piece of land in British Columbia years later, and everyone thought my stepfather was a swell guy, even Mom. But that first unveiling would define our relationship.

My stepfather took us through so many moves. What was he looking for? We changed locations annually before reaching Alaska; the last move before embarking to BC. I started school in a new place every year. Anyone who has had this experience knows it produces an advanced adaptive instinct to where one can define what it takes to blend and overcome being the "new kid" in record time. I hesitate to use the word chameleon because that would imply something shallow or nefarious. Whereas this is basic self-preservation and a simple desire not to have to fight someone at every recess on the schoolyard. One can rightfully say it develops courage and confidence. Regularly engaging new people can broaden knowledge and give appreciation of different perspectives. But I noticed myself getting cautious about forming long-term friendships. The angst of the first few times you say goodbye forever is enough to make you hold back just a little from going "all in" on a new friendship. This was long before the internet, Facebook, or Twitter, and leaving without a forwarding address was really goodbye.

It was in Alaska that I finally got two school years in a row. Eleven years old, in love, with solid friends, and no one called me "Cheechako" anymore; this was when my stepfather dropped the news that we were moving to Canada. He had taken a hunting trip to BC, and read a book called, "How to Get Out of the Rat Race and Live on $10 a Month." He wanted a large piece of land and had heard about the Canadian government still offering agricultural leases, the last vestige of the homestead. Our family gathered its cumulative courage, and for better or worse, we purchased a 3-ton moving truck and a fifth-wheel travel trailer and immigrated to Canada on a southbound trek down the old Alcan Highway, through Dawson Creek.

A circuitous path landed our clan on a 500-acre plot of land in the Hazelton area with 2.4km of river frontage on the Bulkley River near the mouth of the Suskwa River. I say clan because at this point my younger half-brother Adam is part of the crew, a kind and gentle soul, seven years my junior. I say plot of land, because it was exactly that, no road, no power, no buildings, and certainly no indoor plumbing. A remote parcel purchased from famous Sasquatch hunter Bob Titmus. Gloriously beautiful, the field was backed by enormous marshlands visited by thousands of migrating birds annually. The Bulkley's ancient flood waters had terraced half our land into naturally formed wooded flats. The arduous task of converting our small piece of wilderness into a livable working farm began.

What transpired really cannot quantify properly in anything short of a book of its own. It starts with a road, an outhouse, and a shack to live in; get used to the shack. It then rolls non-stop into land clearing, and building a barn, corral, shop, chicken coup, garden plot, hydro project, and miles of fences. All of this built using what is on the land as much as possible, because it's seventy-five km to the nearest big town. If your determination and courage hold out, and you are incredibly lucky, you get to build a proper house to live in before you die. We did it in only nine years. Would have made a great reality TV show, except this was the '70s and reality happened unscripted all on its own without spectators. This experience enriched my life beyond measure. Every day was a lesson in resourcefulness and overcoming adversity. It taught me to work on that which can change and not to worry about what cannot. You only have one life force with which to work. It would have been nothing but a positive experience, but an ugly spectre loomed in the background.

My stepfather's dark side began coming out with growing frequency once we arrived in BC. Not that his base personality changed, I think he just quit filtering when it wasn't necessary. I don't know if it dawned on him that I shared the vision of what the place could be and that death threats, busted teeth, and verbal abuse were not necessary or even warranted. One thing was clear, he was kind, even sweet, to my mother and brother most of the time. His problem was with me, the bastard son. A word I grew to hate. However, I was smarter than he was, especially when he was angry, and learned to cajole and manage him without him knowing it. Usually, if things were done expeditiously, he was OK, even pleasant. But on days when things went wrong, he could be extremely dangerous. I did my time and left my brother and mother in good order. But I hadn't anticipated that after I'd left, he'd simply pick another target. Because I thought I was the problem. Why do we transfer other's problems on ourselves? Eventually I would have to return and stand between him and my brother and mother. But that would occur a couple of years after that day on the road.

Returning to that early morning on the on the side of the road nearly forty years ago, while the fuel had been evaporating from my clothing, my brain had been processing the situation, weighing pros and cons. Two weeks prior it had cost me $1000 to repair a breaking disc that was damaged while I was plowing one of our river fields. It was the lion's share of my summer's savings, but I wasn't leaving owing my stepfather anything. Tallying in the recent loss of half a tank of fuel, if I continued to Vancouver, I would arrive flat broke and living in my car.

The safest thing to do was to turn around now and try to save up for another attempt to leave. I had friends that would put me up for a couple of weeks while I found a place. I had done some temporary work at the mill, and they would probably take me back. But my last day working at the mill was cleaning up an accident. Officially, they called it an accident, but that is not what I saw. It was suicide by log handling equipment. The coroner had cleaned up almost all of it, but I still found tiny bits that were decidedly human. It's something you can't unsee. He was not a close friend, but I had known the man. The only one of the mill crowd running an even keel was the old millwright. Where would I fall in with this crowd? What's more I would still be too close to my stepfather. I was recognizing behaviors of his that I was picking up and it was scaring the hell out of me. Would I resume my Exodus, or still be right here in five years? Everything about this future was unwritten.

When trying to make paramount decisions like this one there are often many inner voices cluttering the path to the right decision. Voices of fear, caution, ego, or intellect are all vying to be heard. Amongst the clamour, there is one voice that is true, if you have the courage to hear it. On that day I heard only one voice telling me to continue my Exodus. I took one last westward look to say goodbye, then climbed back in my car to drive towards an undetermined future, feeling both terrified and exhilarated at the same time.

Nowadays, my age and statis among my peers has often meant I'm asked to start the Thanksgiving, "What I am Thankful for" speeches. I always lead off with, "I am thankful to have survived my youth." It usually gets a few laughs. Except among my close friends, I get a somber look and knowing nod. They were there, too.

ERIC SHARP

Eric Sharp is currently residing in Beaverton, Oregon, United States, and working as an engineer in Research and Development in RV, marine, and portable power products. He grew up on a farm hewn from the wilderness in the Hazelton, British Columbia, Canada area. He spent some years as a mechanic and shop owner in Vancouver, BC. Canada, before returning to the U.S. to attain a degree at UC Berkeley. Eric has strived in his engineering career to find means to produce the products we need without the continued decimation of our planet's environment.

Eric finds fulfillment in helping friends, family, and others overcome adversity, particularly arising from broken or battered childhoods, and allowing them to pursue happiness. He enjoys discovering new locations and meeting new people and has a penchant for road trips without set timelines or itineraries.

Connect with Eric at https://www.facebook.com/sharperic.

The True Heroes

Gabriela Silberhorn

"Courage is not the absence of fear, courage is fear with a prayer." (unknown)

I sat in the car and cried. I was nauseous and despair was rising inside me. I parked in front of the nursing home where my mother was staying. One hour earlier, the nursing home management of the senior center had shown me the section where my mother had to move to. It was the closed area for residents who could run away. They called the area something milder, the sheltered ward. My mother's condition, still physically fit for her age of eighty-four, had been deteriorating the last few weeks. Her advancing dementia made the move necessary. The very attractively furnished, accessible area of the home was where she was currently still occupying a nice room. The only mild dementia was not yet as noticeable in most of the residents. The ward was no different from a general senior center. But my mother had already left the senior center several times in the last few weeks and had not found her way back. She wanted to go home ... our home, where I had grown up.

In the sheltered section, the garden and living areas are not accessible from the outside. The image of the locked windows on the first floor, the outer door with a numerical code lock and the highly fenced garden were still in my mind. Just like the residents of this area. Confused looks, partly empty eyes, physically active residents clamped in walkers so they couldn't run into anything and hurt themselves and others. My sensitive nose still remembered the sour smell of urine, which the scent of cleaning agents could not conceal. Decorative embellishments to the area in the rooms and hallway were not present. Personal items belonging to residents in the rooms were also completely absent. Relatives did not bring anything decorative because the personal items kept disappearing in other rooms or getting broken. No ill intent on the part of the residents, they didn't know any better.

But it was clean, the staff appeared to me to be cordial and empathetic. According to the home's management, the caregivers also took a lot of time with the residents. It became clear to me with this visit how the course of this insidious disease would continue. I had signed. That we children agreed to the move. I had no choice. At home, she would need 24-hour care, and even that could be a risk. The last time she had tried to walk from the home to her old residence, the police had picked her up on a busy street, in the middle of summer, at thirty-five degrees in the shade.

Tomorrow morning, I would leave for the long-planned vacation to Italy to climb at Lake Garda. I had to take the decision and the picture with me. My sister would accompany the move.

I had been sitting in the car for half an hour, tears still running down my cheeks. How was I going to make it. Seeing my mother in this area would break my heart. A nightmare of the last few months compounded. "What else God," I said aloud. "What else" helplessness overcame me. Panic constricted my throat. I felt nauseous. No help. I started the engine. I drove home and packed my things. That evening, I consciously began to pray for this situation, for my mother, and for myself and my siblings. Praying and meditating is part of my daily habits and had always helped me so far. It had always shown me a way to deal with the pain and anxiety.

The next morning, I loaded my luggage, tied my bike to the rack on the car and took off. Off to the south. The annual highlight in Europe for climbers, the Rockmaster event at Lake Garda awaited me and my friends in Arco. The place that was like a second home to me. Good climbers from all over the world, as well as many climbing enthusiasts like me would meet in the idyllic, typical Italian place. So, distraction was guaranteed. Slowly joy came up in me. "I can do this" I thought. I also managed to vacation here with friends again last year after my separation from my ex-husband. The first time after he moved out three years ago. At that time, I had the feeling of a new beginning. Maybe the whole scenario, the aliveness embedded in the Italian charm, will help me to accept the fact of my mother's mental decline. Both exists in this world, and both has their place and justification. Even if I could not understand why. Why do people have to go this way. A small comfort was the statement from my coach. Dementia is a family disease. Those affected don't suffer as much as the family members who watch.

It was true. When I asked my mother how she was doing, she always confirmed very clearly that she was fine.

Every evening I took time to ask heaven, God, the angels or whatever we want to call it, to give me the strength and courage to face the situation when I was back home.

Arco distracted me. The sports and climbing community at the competition as much as the climbing on the rock. Every day I was consciously grateful for my body and my mind. What a gift both were. As I sat at the base of the climbing crag quietly contemplating the beautiful landscape, I thought of how finite all of this was. And how more fulfilled we would feel if we could view life in the context of this finitude. Sometimes I succeeded, and a deep love and gratitude for life rose within me. For the infinite possibilities that life can hold for us. I could not yet hold this awareness permanently.

I realized that most of my fear was not fear for my mother alone. It was my own fear of finitude, of losing everything that gave me joy. For the past few years, I've had to deal with health projects. I panicked that my own health would continue to deteriorate. That I would end up in that home. My throat immediately tightened, and my stomach cramped again at that thought.

It was interesting. I watched others climb steep walls and overhangs. I felt the excitement inside me when I hung from hooks fixed in the rock at dizzying heights of thirty to sixty meters, secured only by rope. I could also stand up in front of more than one hundred people in my job as a trainer and speaker if I had to, and spray motivation. On so many occasions I moved safely and routinely, without thinking, where many others would hold their breath. In contrast, the thought of visiting my mother, having to face physical and mental deterioration, choked me up. My hands began to shake. I closed my eyes, breathed in the fresh air and the energy of the rocks and nature, prayed silently again, and asked for guidance and healing.

The vacation flew by, and I started my journey home with a queasy feeling. Not much had changed in terms of my fear of encountering the home. But I was more refreshed and powerful.

So, the day came when I sat in the car in the same parking lot and focused on my breathing. My fear of facing the same fate as my mother caused dizziness in me. The idea of losing all my joy, of feeling only darkness, brought tears to my eyes again. So did seeing that it was already like that for my mother now. I took another deep breath and got out of the car. My sister was already waiting at the entrance of the retirement home. I greeted her but could not hug her. Otherwise, I would have lost my composure. She looked at me with understanding. She had felt the same way on her first visit to the new ward. We entered the care home. We opened the door to the protected area with the numerical code and I followed my sister. I closed my eyes briefly and asked my angels and all other heavenly companions for help.

When I opened my eyes again, I saw her. My mother. She was sitting in the small dining room at the head of the table, like a boss. Behind her stood a plump attendant who radiated warmth and affection. She stroked my mother's shoulders and upper back with both hands. They both swayed in time to the music playing softly in the background. My mother had a beatific expression on her face. Physical touch had been difficult for her to accept in the past. I could not remember experiencing many hugs as a child. She only allowed hugs after my father died ten years ago. Before that, she always maintained a physical distance from her environment. I lived the opposite.

Then she saw us. Her eyes lit up. She had recognized us. Thank you, angel, I thought. That look was compensation for all the fear I had to overcome, which was still choking my throat. Tears rose in me, this time of relief. For my mother. And for me. She so obviously enjoyed the companionship and closeness of the nurse. Something she herself had never experienced like this in her childhood. Her parents considered their children a burden and expressed it that way to her and her siblings. If you knew my grandparents' story, you understood why. Still, for my mother, it was a deep wound. 'Which may be allowed to heal here,' I thought. I walked up to her and hugged her. I felt her warmth and realized that her hug had changed. She was hugging me much tighter than usual. The caregiver smiled warmly at me. "Your mother is already settling in well," she said to us.

I saw the caregivers busily feeding people coffee and cake. A few were being fed. The person sitting next to my mother smiled at me. It was her roommate. A 104-year-old friendly lady. Then my sister picked up my mother's coat and we walked together with her to the adjacent park. The three of us sat side by side on a bench and silently looked at nature and the birds. "Look at the beautiful clouds," my mother interrupted the silence. "As children we used to watch the clouds and say what we see." Then she laughed. She saw an elephant. I grinned. I saw a dwarf by another cloud. My sister an angel. As we took her back to her area, I thought about my vacation. Of the climbing competition. How much courage all those admirable athletes lived day after day, winning against gravity. I thought of Alex Honnold, an American climber by which I was amazed. He had climbed a 1000-meter rock face on El Capitan in Yosemite Valley free solo, that is, without belaying. At a difficulty level where I was not able to come even two meters off the ground. Which meant not at all with my height of 1.68 meters. Heroic and certainly very admirable, how these climbers went to their physical and mental limits and accomplished masterpieces.

But the people who worked here, and somehow also the residents, those were my real heroes. The residents because their soul took this path in their lives, for whatever reason. Perhaps because if you looked closely, they show us that even here, life still makes sense. And the caregivers, people who shone as a light with warmth and love in this seeming suffering. Even if they don't draw much attention to themselves. Silent heroes.

And I saw my courageous first step in facing my fear about the transience of my body and mind. I embraced my courage, even though I suspected I still had a way to go here. But like climbing, it's always step by step. Even with a 1000-meter-high rock face, this is the only way to reach the top.

NOTE: This chapter was originally written in German and then translated into English. We invited the author, Gabriela Silberhorn, to share the German version, which you'll see on the following pages after her bio.

GABRIELA SILBERHORN

Gabriela Silberhorn grew up in beautiful Bavaria, Germany, where she still lives.

Due to her own challenges, life led her back deeper and deeper into the connection to the heart. Who am I and what do I want? Two questions that have preoccupied her since the age of twelve and have accompanied her throughout her life. Now, at the age of over fifty, she is beginning to recreate herself once again, to develop new potentials and to redefine her values and her orientation in life. As a trained banker, she currently supports her boss in his medium-sized company in the healthcare sector as a coach and personnel developer for the employees, as well as in the areas of finance and marketing. In her own small business, she offers spiritual art in the form of acrylic paintings such as mandalas, energy, and angel paintings and mandala stones. Her artistic and creative vein was laid in her cradle by her parents. This gift also helps her in daily life and in her job to find creative solutions. New in her life is the writing work as an author. She has started authoring a new book in the form of a novel to express her life story and insights in a light and entertaining form. A new experience is also to write in English and not in German as usual.

Her vision is to help people reconnect with their heart and intuition to live a fuller and happier life, despite all our earthly challenges.

Connect with Gabriela at www.energieundengelwelt.de.

Die wahren Helden

(Unedited German Version)

von Gabriela Silberhorn

"Mut ist nicht die Abwesenheit von Angst, Mut ist Angst die gebetet hat." (unbekannt)

Ich saß im Auto und weinte. Mir war übel und Verzweiflung stieg in mir auf. Ich parkte vor dem Pflegeheim, in dem meine Mutter untergebracht war. Eine Stunde zuvor hatte mir die Heimleitung des Seniorenzentrums den Bereich gezeigt, in den meine Mutter umziehen musste. Es war der geschlossene Bereich für Bewohner, die weglaufen konnten. Sie nannten die Abteilung etwas milder, die behütete Station. Der Zustand meiner Mutter, die für ihr Alter von vierundachtzig Jahren körperlich noch fit war, hatte sich in den letzten Wochen verschlechtert. Ihre fortschreitende Demenz machte den Umzug notwendig. In dem sehr ansprechend eingerichteten, offenen Bereich des Heims bewohnte sie derzeit noch ein schönes Zimmer. Die nur leichte Demenz war bei den meisten Bewohnern noch nicht so auffällig. Diese Station unterschied sich auf den ersten Blick nicht so sehr von einem allgemeinen Seniorenzentrum. Aber meine Mutter hatte das Seniorenwohnheim in den letzten Wochen schon mehrmals verlassen und den Weg zurück nicht mehr gefunden. Sie wollte nach Hause ... unser Zuhause, in dem ich aufgewachsen war.

In der behüteten Station sind der Garten und die Wohnbereiche nicht von außen zugänglich. Das Bild der verschlossenen Fenster im ersten Stock, der Außentür mit einem Zahlencode-Schloss und des hoch eingezäunten Gartens hatte ich noch im Kopf. Genau wie die Bewohner dieses Bereiches. Verwirrte Blicke, teilweise leere Augen, körperlich aktive Bewohner, die in Gehwägen eingespannt waren, damit sie nirgends hinrennen und sich und andere verletzen konnten. Meine empfindliche Nase erinnerte sich noch an den leicht säuerlichen Geruch von Urin, den auch der Duft von Reinigungsmitteln nicht überdecken konnte. Dekorative Verschönerungen des Bereiches in den Zimmern und auf dem Flur waren nicht viele vorhanden. Auch persönliche Gegenstände der Bewohner in den Zimmern fehlten fast völlig. Angehörige brachten nichts Dekoratives mit, weil die persönlichen Gegenstände immer wieder in anderen Zimmern verschwanden oder kaputt gingen. Die Bewohnerinnen und Bewohner hatten keine böse Absicht, sie wussten es nicht besser.

Aber es war sauber, das Personal erschien mir herzlich und einfühlsam. Nach Angaben der Heimleitung nahmen sich die Betreuer viel Zeit für die Bewohner. Bei diesem Besuch wurde mir klar, wie der Verlauf dieser heimtückischen Krankheit weitergehen würde.

Ich hatte unterschrieben. Dass wir Kinder dem Umzug zustimmten. Ich hatte keine andere Wahl. Zu Hause würde sie rund um die Uhr betreut werden müssen, und selbst das könnte ein Risiko sein. Beim letzten Versuch, vom Heim zu ihrem alten Wohnort zu laufen, hatte die Polizei sie auf einer belebten Straße aufgegriffen. Mitten im Hochsommer, bei 35 Grad im Schatten.

Am nächsten Tag würde ich in den lang geplanten Urlaub nach Italien aufbrechen, um am Gardasee zu klettern. Ich musste die Entscheidung und das Bild mitnehmen. Meine Schwester würde den Umzug begleiten.

Ich saß schon seit einer halben Stunde im Auto, die Tränen liefen mir immer noch über die Wangen. Wie sollte ich das nur schaffen?

Meine Mutter in diesem Bereich zu sehen, würde mir das Herz brechen. Der Albtraum der letzten Monate steigerte sich tatsächlich. "Was noch, Gott", sagte ich laut. "Was noch!" Hilflosigkeit überkam mich. Panik schnürte mir die Kehle zu. Am liebsten hätte ich mich übergeben. Es half nichts. Ich startete den Motor, fuhr nach Hause und packte meine Sachen. An diesem Abend begann ich bewusst für diese Situation zu beten, für meine Mutter und für mich und meine Geschwister. Beten und Meditieren gehört zu meinen täglichen Gewohnheiten und hatte mir bisher immer geholfen. Es hatte mir immer einen Weg gezeigt, mit dem Schmerz und der Angst umzugehen.

Am nächsten Morgen lud ich mein Gepäck ein, befestigte mein Fahrrad auf dem Gepäckträger des Autos und fuhr los. Ab in den Süden. Das jährliche Highlight in Europa für Kletterer, das Rockmaster Event am Gardasee, erwartete mich und meine Freunde in Arco. Der Ort, der für mich wie eine zweite Heimat war. In dem idyllischen, typisch italienischen Ort trafen sich gute Kletterer aus der ganzen Welt und viele Kletterbegeisterte wie ich. Ablenkung war dort also garantiert. Langsam kam Freude in mir auf. "Ich schaffe das", dachte ich. Auch letztes Jahr habe ich es geschafft, nach der Trennung von meinem Ex-Mann hier wieder mit Freunden Urlaub zu machen. Das erste Mal, nachdem er zwei Jahre zuvor ausgezogen war. Damals hatte ich das Gefühl eines Neuanfangs. Vielleicht hilft mir das ganze Szenario, die Lebendigkeit eingebettet in den italienischen Charme, dabei, die Tatsache des geistigen Verfalls meiner Mutter zu akzeptieren. Beides existiert auf dieser Welt, und beides hat seinen Platz und seine Berechtigung. Auch wenn ich nicht verstehen konnte, warum. Warum müssen Menschen diesen Weg gehen. Ein kleiner Trost war die Aussage meiner Coachin. Demenz ist eine Angehörigenkrankheit. Die Betroffenen leiden nicht so sehr wie die Familienmitglieder, die zusehen. Es stimmte. Wenn ich meine Mutter fragte, wie es ihr geht, bestätigte sie immer sehr deutlich, dass es ihr gut geht.

Jeden Abend nahm ich mir Zeit, den Himmel, Gott, die Engel oder wie auch immer wir es nennen wollen, zu bitten, mir die Kraft und den Mut zu geben. Dafür, wenn ich der Situation zu Hause ins Auge schauen musste.

Arco lenkte mich ab. Die Sport- und Klettergemeinschaft beim Wettkampf ebenso wie das Klettern am Fels. Jeden Tag nahm ich dankbar ganz bewusst meinen Körper und meinen Geist wahr. Was für ein Geschenk beides war. Als ich am Fuße des Kletterfelsens saß und die wunderschöne Landschaft still betrachtete, dachte ich darüber nach, wie endlich das alles ist. Und wie viel erfüllter wir uns fühlen würden, wenn wir das Leben im Kontext dieser Endlichkeit betrachten könnten. Manchmal gelang mir das, und eine tiefe Liebe und Dankbarkeit für das Leben stieg dann in mir auf. Für die unendlichen Möglichkeiten, die das Leben für uns bereithalten kann. Dauerhaft konnte ich dieses Bewusstsein noch nicht halten.

Mir wurde klar, dass der größte Teil meiner Angst nicht alleine die Angst um meine Mutter war. Es war meine eigene Angst. Vor der Endlichkeit. Vor dem Verlust all dessen, was mir Freude machte. In den letzten Jahren musste ich mich mit gesundheitlichen Projekten auseinandersetzen. Ich hatte Panik, dass sich meine eigene Gesundheit weiter verschlechtern würde. Dass ich selbst in einem Heim enden würde. Bei diesem Gedanken schnürte es mir sofort wieder die Kehle zu und mein Magen verkrampfte.

Es war interessant. Ich sah anderen beim Klettern in Steilwänden und in Überhängen zu. Spürte die Begeisterung in mir, wenn ich selbst in schwindelnder Höhe von 30 bis 60 Metern nur mit Seil gesichert an im Fels befestigten Haken hing. Auch in meinem Job als Trainerin und Rednerin konnte ich, wenn es sein musste, vor mehr als hundert Menschen stehen und Motivation versprühen. Bei so vielen Gelegenheiten bewegte ich mich sicher und routiniert, ohne nachzudenken, wo viele andere den Atem anhalten würden. Der Gedanke daran, meine

Mutter zu besuchen und mit ihrem körperlichen und geistigen Verfall konfrontiert zu werden, ließ mich dagegen erstarren. Meine Hände begannen zu zittern. Ich schloss meine Augen und atmete die frische Luft und die Energie der Felsen und der Natur ein. Ich betete wieder still und bat um Führung und Heilung.

Der Urlaub verging wie im Flug und ich trat die Heimreise mit einem mulmigen Gefühl an. In Bezug auf meine Angst vor der Begegnung im Heim hatte sich nicht viel geändert. Aber ich fühlte mich erfrischt und kraftvoll.

So kam der Tag, an dem ich im Auto auf demselben Parkplatz saß und mich auf meinen Atem konzentrierte. Meine Angst, das gleiche Schicksal wie meine Mutter zu erleiden, verursachte Schwindelgefühle in mir. Die Vorstellung, all meine Freude zu verlieren und nur noch Dunkelheit zu spüren, trieb mir erneut Tränen in die Augen. Genauso wie der Gedanke, dass es meiner Mutter schon jetzt so ging. Ich holte noch einmal tief Luft und stieg aus dem Auto aus. Meine Schwester wartete bereits am Eingang des Seniorenwohnheims. Ich begrüßte sie, konnte sie aber nicht umarmen. Sonst hätte ich die Fassung verloren. Sie sah mich verständnisvoll an. So hatte sie sich bei ihrem ersten Besuch in der neuen Station auch gefühlt. Wir betraten das Pflegeheim. Wir öffneten die Tür zum geschützten Bereich mit dem Zahlencode und ich folgte meiner Schwester. Ich schloss kurz die Augen und bat meine Engel und alle anderen himmlischen Gefährten um Hilfe.

Als ich meine Augen wieder öffnete, sah ich sie. Meine Mutter. Sie saß in dem kleinen Speisesaal am Kopfende des Tisches, wie eine Chefin. Hinter ihr stand eine mollige Betreuerin, die Wärme und herzliche Zuneigung ausstrahlte. Sie streichelte mit beiden Händen über die Schultern und den oberen Rücken meiner Mutter. Beide wippten im Takt der Musik, die leise im Hintergrund lief. Meine Mutter hatte einen seligen Gesichtsausdruck. Körperliche Berührungen waren für sie in der Vergangenheit schwer zu akzeptieren gewesen. Ich konnte mich nicht erinnern, dass ich als Kind viele Umarmungen erlebt hatte. Sie erlaubte Umarmungen erst, nachdem mein Vater vor zehn Jahren gestorben war. Davor pflegte sie immer eine körperliche Distanz zu ihrer Umgebung. Ich lebte das Gegenteil.

Dann sah sie uns. Ihre Augen leuchteten auf. Sie hatte uns erkannt. Danke, Engel, dachte ich. Dieser Blick war eine Entschädigung für all die Angst, die ich überwinden musste und die mir immer noch im Hals steckte. Tränen stiegen in mir auf, dieses Mal vor Erleichterung. Für meine Mutter. Und für mich. Sie genoss so offensichtlich die Gesellschaft und Nähe der Betreuerin. Etwas, das sie selbst in ihrer Kindheit nie so erlebt hatte. Ihre Eltern betrachteten ihre Kinder als Last und drückten das auch ihr und ihren Geschwistern gegenüber so aus. Wenn man die Geschichte meiner Großeltern kennt, versteht man, warum. Doch für meine Mutter war es dennoch eine tiefe Wunde. „Die hier vielleicht heilen darf", dachte ich. Ich ging auf sie zu und umarmte sie. Ich spürte ihre Wärme und merkte, dass sich ihre Umarmung verändert hatte. Sie drückte mich deutlich fester als sonst. Die Betreuerin lächelte mich herzlich an. "Ihre Mutter hat sich schon gut eingelebt", sagte sie zu uns.

Ich sah, dass die Pflegerinnen und Pfleger eifrig dabei waren, die Leute mit Kaffee und Kuchen zu versorgen. Ein paar wurden gerade gefüttert. Die Person, die neben meiner Mutter saß, lächelte mich an. Es war ihre Zimmermitbewohnerin. Eine 104-jährige freundliche Dame. Dann holte meine Schwester den Mantel meiner Mutter und wir gingen gemeinsam mit ihr in den angrenzenden Park. Zu dritt setzten wir uns nebeneinander auf eine Bank und betrachteten schweigend die Natur und die Vögel. "Schau dir die schönen Wolken an", unterbrach meine Mutter die Stille. "Als Kinder haben wir immer die Wolken beobachtet und gesagt, was wir sehen." Dann lachte sie. Sie sah einen Elefanten. Ich grinste. Ich sah bei einer anderen Wolke einen Zwerg. Meine Schwester einen Engel. Als wir sie zurück in ihren Wohnbereich brachten, dachte ich an meinen Urlaub. An den Kletterwettbewerb. Wie viel Mut all diese bewundernswerten Athleten Tag für Tag lebten und gegen die Schwerkraft gewannen. Ich dachte an Alex Honnold, einen amerikanischen Kletterer, von dem ich begeistert war. Er hatte eine 1000 Meter hohe Felswand am El Capitan im Yosemite Valley im Alleingang, free solo, d.h. ohne Sicherung, durchgeklettert. In einem Schwierigkeitsgrad, in dem ich nicht einmal zwei Meter vom Boden abhob. Bei meiner Körpergröße von 1,68 m hieß das also „gar nicht". Heldenhaft und sicherlich sehr bewundernswert, wie diese Kletterer an ihre körperlichen und mentalen Grenzen gingen und Meisterleistungen vollbrachten.

Doch die Menschen, die hier arbeiteten, und irgendwie auch die Bewohner, das waren meine wahren Helden. Die Bewohner, weil ihre Seele diesen Weg in ihrem Leben eingeschlagen hat, aus welchem Grund auch immer. Vielleicht weil sie uns, wenn man genau hinsieht, zeigen, dass das Leben auch hier noch einen Sinn hat. Und die Pflegekräfte, Menschen, die in diesem scheinbaren Leid wie ein Licht mit Wärme und Liebe leuchteten. Auch wenn sie nicht viel Aufmerksamkeit auf sich ziehen. Stille Helden.

Und ich sah meinen ersten mutigen Schritt, mich meiner Angst vor der Vergänglichkeit meines Körpers und Geistes zu stellen. Ich umarmte meinen Mut, auch wenn ich ahnte, dass ich noch einen weiten Weg vor mir hatte. Aber wie beim Klettern geht es immer Schritt für Schritt. Selbst bei einer 1000 Meter hohen Felswand ist das der einzige Weg, um den Gipfel zu erreichen.

The Courage to Empower

Helena Wall

"It takes courage to grow up and become who you really are."
~E.E. Cummings

I was born into a family where tradition and religion were intermingled, with no clear distinction between the two. Truly, it was the only way of being that I knew. So many things were fearsome. God was ever-watchful, judging, and condemning. We were seven daughters who most certainly squabbled. Mom often said, "bad girls don't go to heaven." In one of my most memorable dreams, we were all gathered on a beach when God called my name. God told me to "go away from me, for you do not belong in the kingdom." I tried to convince myself it was not me that was being sent away, but instead someone else who shared my name. I still remember how it felt and I longed with all my heart that I would make it to adulthood. I reasoned in my child-mind that if that happened, I would be okay at last. I was taught that snakes were evil, and if seen, it was our duty to kill them. I had nightmares. I was terrified of the thunderstorms that were God's way of expressing his anger with us. Whether day or night, we all sat and listened with hands folded in our laps, waiting for the storm to pass. I sat really close to my mother and would have gladly merged into her body. I had Dad on the one hand expressing that God was angry, and Mom offering the only solace she could, saying that God would only let happen what he would allow. In time, I was able to release the terror. I did know God to be all-knowing and all-powerful with absolute faith.

Young girls and boys attended a one-room school and learned reading from religious texts, moving from an introductory reader called the Fieble, then Catechism, up to the New Testament, and eventually, the Bible. When girls reached the age of puberty, they were considered finished with school and at about the same age the boys were soon ready to go to work with their fathers on their farm or in business.

My parents moved the family to Canada in 1974. This was my father's attempt to get away from the grind of working from before sun-up until after dark. We trekked via coach bus through the continental United States to get from Mexico to Canada.

We were in a country that would have naturalized us all, had my mother not been born here in 1944. Had she been born in 1947 or later, she would have been considered a citizen. Thirty years later, this law was still being enforced.

I was just shy of being eight years old and began school in Canada, learning language, reading, and writing all at the same time. I enjoyed learning. Alternatively, my two older sisters who had been harassed in school decided to stop going at the end of grade six.

Schoolmates harassed me, too, but I pressed on. I was not going to forgo an education just to avoid the abuse for being "Mexican."

In time, however, my parents decided that I should end my academic career and quit school. Technically, it was time for me to attend high school, another evil to be afraid of. Soon after I had started a job, my parents and I were invited to attend a meeting with the school board. I told them I really wanted to go to school. My parents were told that they had to allow me to go until I was sixteen, and then to let me decide.

A friend at school informed me that I could tap into a support program that would allow me to continue my schooling even if my parents wouldn't allow me to live at home. I took this information to them, and my mother took a stand for me. This was a rare thing for a faithful wife to be doing. What she said to me was that she would never tell a child of hers that they could not live at home. Whatever she said to Dad, it happened outside of my hearing. He dropped the fight. By this time, Dad had eased off on the corporal punishments in the family. I don't know why, but I have wondered about this. He had, at one time, in an out-of-control rage, beaten one of my sisters (alcohol may have been a factor for him). She stayed home from school for a period while her bruises healed. I imagine someone warned him that people in Canada can lose their children for this.

I continued to go until the end of high school, enduring the sometimes-hostile environments. A guidance counselor at the school convinced me that I must go on; he saw greatness in my future. When I graduated, he said he'd never been prouder of any student. I got a university degree in something I found interesting, with no clear end goal in mind. As I graduated, I was unfocused and in need of change from the classroom. Before long, I met my husband and settled down. I carried the responsibility of holding down a regular job which my partner struggled to maintain. The desire to pursue something more was alive, but reality argued against this.

I found myself in a long-term position in human-support services, reasoning to myself that my parents could hardly find fault in such a career. The sense that I had more in me was never far away. With all the fight it had taken for me to become educated, I had still limited my choices in an effort to avoid having them angry with me. I had settled for less than my true calling.

I learned so much in my line of work, and I learned of aspects of life in a way that deviated from my upbringing.

One powerful influence was the regular training in Nonviolent Crisis Intervention (NVCI). I passionately cared about the treatment of others, especially those in the vulnerable sector. I was using nonviolent approaches when addressing behavior crises. I have the sort of mind that loves to take a complex thing and make it simple. I came to recognize that violence as an intervention approach was something unnecessary and deeply abhorrent to me. I could relate to being vulnerable, after having my peers harass me in school simply for being "different," in a way that I had no control over. Resorting to violence as an intervention technique is a strong impulse when it has been part of one's upbringing. It became truly clear to me that it was something that I was not willing to tolerate as part of my life.

One day I was chatting with a friend about the relationship struggles I encountered with my young daughter. My friend mentioned a name that caught my attention, one that I came to have profound respect for, Dr. Marshall Rosenberg. Dr. Rosenberg developed a style of communication called Nonviolent Communication. Some proponents of his work have dubbed it Compassionate Communication. What's interesting to me is its similarities, on a verbal plane, to the physical approaches of NVCI. It's interesting how strongly his work resonated with me, as I dove into personal study of his material, ordering the course, books, and watching hours of videos on YouTube.

I shared that the culture I was born into was oppressive in terms of limiting personal freedoms. It is a religion known for pacifism and adult baptism, done at an age when a person chooses of their own free will to join the faith. I resonate with pacifism and personal freedom both. It diverges where the church dictates the nature of the faith. Symbolic aspects of life are interpreted literally and oppress rather than empower individuals, especially females.

At the much more liberated Spiritualist Church, my spirit rests in the freedom of using what is useful to me, and gently setting aside that which doesn't resonate with me at any given time. No one is condemned for their beliefs, and no one fears burning in an eternal hell.

It boils down to nonviolence. And it's about authenticity, truly, through a process of deep personal discernment. There is one path that I must walk alone.

With a rich history of fearfulness bred into my child-psyche, I came to recognize that my emotional state was anxious, and bordered on psychotic, or at least neurotic. I was so sad it worried me. I thought deeply about it and began to search for things that felt light. When I became aware of a catastrophe, I looked for happy things to focus on. To my delight, I found plenty! I came to realize that to feel okay, I could make it my deliberate choice to put my attention on the things that were neutral or happy, even extending the neutral to the realms of "happy." No one told me about universal laws. I became somewhat of a self-taught competent.

How have I grown from there? This is an ever-evolving process. If you can imagine, the religion/culture taught me to remain small, unseen, and powerless. Men were the decision-making heads of households. Never was I encouraged by those around me to aspire to make anything of my life beyond being a wife and mother. Add a generous layer of the philosophy of money being rooted in evil, and the pursuit of a destiny was never even spoken of. My elders told me to take care of others, but never once did I hear, "take care of yourself."

Thus, it meant that I would need to make it my own responsibility to not focus on feelings of sadness, despair, and hopelessness. The "good girl" version of me wanted my parents to be happy, or at least content with me. Yet, I knew in my core that I could not deny myself simply to please them. Hence, I compromised. I was not yet at the stage of allowing myself the privilege to truly venture forth, unapologetic, completely healed of my people-pleaser co-dependent self, a legitimate product of the alcoholism present in my family history. As I have taken a personal journey of recovery, I have concluded that addiction is profuse in untold grief and tragedy. The miracle of recovery in 12-step rooms is the progression beyond these. In my further studies with a mentor and support coaches, I have borne witness to the creation of a new self-identity, one beyond addiction.

I came to realize that, for me, relationships are the most important thing in life. Like everyone, I wanted happiness, whatever that meant to me. It sometimes meant taking the higher path to keep peace, and sometimes compromising my position on an issue. As I've grown more self-confident in my convictions around my core values, I have also learned to stand my ground peacefully, kindly, and firmly. I own my choices in life.

In the process of writing this chapter, the truth of constant unfolding and deeper and deeper insights is very present. I'm reminded that this is as life is designed to be on Earth. The more that I am leaning into the natural process, the more powerful I become in designing my own experience. I also get to be playful and experimental with it, to create joyful sensations for myself and to help others learn to trust in the process, too, and to design life as they wish it to be for them.

"When all is said and done, we are all just walking each other home"
~ Ram Das

Shall we?

HELENA WALL

Helena Wall is an aspiring new author and entrepreneur, in the process of establishing her own company as an Empowerment Mentor and Consultant.

She was aware of her call to write for many years, and through the years, friends and peers alike asked her when she planned to heed the call. As the world began to approach a new normal following a global pandemic in 2021, Helena found herself leaving the career that spanned the better part of three decades.

She spent several months studying herself while also working for the academy. Then, the realization began to dawn that the environment she was in was not the best fit.

The time to follow her true calling had come! Her awareness had shifted so much! She had grown most in the areas of self-love, self-acceptance, and confidence. As she healed herself, the confusion began to clear and make way for the path forward. She felt so free, so empowered!

The betterment of all life is of keen interest to Helena. She approaches this using various techniques and strategies. Among them are Emotional Freedom Technique (tapping), Nonviolent Communication

(NVC), Nonviolent Crisis Intervention (NVCI), Spirituality, Manifestation, Peak Performance, Mentorship and Leadership.

In her leisure time, Helena enjoys reading, writing, life-long studies, art, music, walks, day trips, and travel.

More than anything else, she cherishes the many relationships in her life. She lives in Kitchener, Canada, with her life partner and their cat.

Connect with Helena at https://linktr.ee/helenawall.

The Resilience Activator: Building a Heart-Mind Connection

Jean Cobine

"The courageous heart shines their radiant light with true acceptance for self and others." ~Jean Cobine

Dear Reader,

Here is a question: do you find yourself reacting or responding to life?

When asked, most people tilt their head to the side and furrow their eyebrows. "Is there a difference?" they wonder. "And more to the point, does how I react to the stressors in my life really matter?"

To this I say, yes! There certainly is a difference. In addition, the methods we use to face challenges in our lives *do* matter. In this chapter, I invite you to join me on a journey of self-discovery. In the following pages, you are going to learn about why being your own resilience activator is – quite possibly – the most important skill a spiritual person can ever hope to master in this lifetime. Our goal is to live a grounded and gentle life. Gentle with the earth, others, and ourselves. To do this, we must build a heart-mind connection. One that is based on our energy and the ways we choose to interact with others.

Ready to begin?

Let us start.

Responding vs. Reacting

First, let me give you two definitions. To frame the work that we will be undertaking, let us start off by clarifying what "responding" is. Responding occurs when you are in power. In situations such as this, you will be actively taking in the unfolding situation (or conversation) and digesting information before you act. Though it may look like you are doing little, this is intentional. It is key to note that saying or doing nothing is still a type of response!

On the other hand, we have reacting. Unlike responding, reacting is when you rush in. A person who is reacting will take no time to think things through. Rather than calmly absorbing what is happening or the messages shared, so-called "reactors" jump straight in with their own thoughts, words, and actions. You yourself may be reading this and thinking, "Hey. That sounds an awful lot like me."

Of course, this can lead to all sorts of problems! After the initial reaction to such stimulus, you take a minute to pause. Reflect on what just happened. Emotions were flying high, anger bubbled to the surface, you expressed unleashed frustration, overwhelming emotion and you are then in an argument. Now, we enter the "reflection" stage. More likely than not, you feel a deep grief. Heck, even a little guilty! When we ignore the "responding" side of our hearts and instead lash out by "reacting," the result is a feeling of unworthiness, powerlessness, and a false belief that you are beyond repair.

If this sounds familiar, do not fret. You are not alone. In fact, I personally experienced burnouts in various chapters of my life and even to this day I am still a work in progress as I navigate my way through, with each potential burnout presenting another layer of learning. Just a couple of years ago, I had been working in a high-pressure role for eight and a half years where when there were staff resignations, rather than replace they shared the tasks amongst existing staff. There was this expectant attitude to accept and 'just do it.' At the time I can recall feeling a sense of self-importance which others validated. Feeling like wonder woman (martyrdom, and strong masculine energy) I reached a point where the 'burn-out' peaked and this is when I came into full realisation that the self-importance came at the cost of what is profoundly important, my wellbeing and family.

Such experiences are a normal part of our growth. For me it was time for massive change! It was time for me to look within and seek self-validation, self-appreciation, and self-worth and it started with getting curious, 'who am I, if I am not this job?' and 'who am I if I am not the role I play?'

The good news is, by reading this chapter, you have committed to becoming more self-aware! This is the first step towards building a strong heart-mind connection. But the bigger question remains…why do we sabotage ourselves (and our relationships) in this way?

Getting Trapped in Destructive Patterns

Sometimes, we react to the needs of others because we feel it is our duty to fix them. No one needs fixing! Everybody just wants acceptance. We all desire the freedom to be happy. Nothing about these needs is abnormal. We are all human. So, why then do we allow emotional outbursts and overreacting behavior to control us? Why do we permit other people to have so much control over our feelings? To illustrate this concept, let us examine a case study. This will highlight how (and why) we get stuck in destructive patterns that stunt our growth.

Consider the Following Imaginary Scenario

A close friend recently lost their job. She comes to you – scared and anxious – seeking advice. With kind intentions, you offer to loan her money. Your friend immediately gets offended. "You think I'm asking for charity?" she snaps. "You are not even listening! I do not need cash. You always want to fix everything!" Suddenly, the conversation has gone off the rails! The misunderstanding escalates. Soon, you are both yelling at one another, trying to be the loudest, and neither party feels heard.

It is a classic case of reacting.

What to Do Instead

When we struggle to regulate in such ways, it can be easier to just call it quits. We wish the earth would crack open and swallow us up, thus dissolving all that has happened. Unfortunately, that is not possible. While we cannot rewind and go back in time, we can wipe the slate clean! We can take a leap of faith. We can choose to entertain a better thought, right there in the moment. First, start with gratitude for your newfound awareness. It has been reawakened. Reactionary behavior is not the end – it is only the beginning of something much, much, better. Ask yourself: what is the next best thing I can do right now?

Listening with the Heart (Not the Head)

Princess Diana once famously said, "Only do what your heart tells you." When we listen to our heart, we can come into our centre. Paying attention to our breath and listening to these whispers of our heart enlightens us to the truth. Be quiet. Close your mouth. Stop "reacting" to things out of your control and instead let your heart guide you in magnificent ways towards "responding" to life with a soft heart, yet strong spine. Only in the silence can we realise that we are not responsible for the choices that others make. However, we can absolutely take radical responsibility for our own lives, our own actions, and our own words. By doing so, we consciously alter our contribution to all our humanity.

And that, dear reader, is nothing short of incredible!

New life emerges when you come into your heart. You feel a sense of calm. At peace. In these moments, you have tapped into your heart and subsequently activated the all-powerful emotional resilience within. Now, you are ready to respond to life. This true response to life and its situations, conversations, and human interactions is the activation of what I like to refer to as your "mind-heart coherence."

Allow me to explain. With a clear-thinking mind, you are in control. Anger dissipates. Fear ebbs away like waves on the sand. Your conscious mind is open. Negative thoughts and emotions no longer overwhelm you. Rather, it is ready to hear your heart…and the hearts of others.

Make no mistake – this is powerful stuff.

Spiritualists and those on a path of self-exploration and personal improvement can spend a lifetime trying to achieve this goal. You, dear reader, are already doing so just by being receptive to this message, your heart's message. Expressing your heartfelt gratitude for this journey to the Divine, the Universe (or whatever feels right for you) will magnify such feelings in your heart to slow down, notice, acknowledge, and feel deeply. From here, all situations, people, and fellow humans feel your response.

Conclusion and Next Steps

Congratulations!

You have landed. You are firmly standing in your power, embracing the truth of who you are while also embodying the whole of you.

There is no longer the fear, the sickly taste of what has come before. You are home!

Feels good, doesn't it?

As we approach the end of our chapter together, it is my sincere hope that you now have the strength, courage, and acceptance to shine your radiant light. Not only as a lantern for yourself in dark times, but also as a beacon for others. A new learning has taken up residence inside of your chest. You have formed pathways from your heart to your brain. You will never return to overreacting. That door has closed. You can hold your head high and face the sun, knowing that you are in the right place, here in your heart, responding to life and all situations and events with only love. A love so pure, it is almost divine.

Understand this: by embracing this divine energy, you are adding value to your world and the whole planet at large. Will it be easy? No. Will it be worth the effort? Yes!

What comes next? Practice. Commitment. A dedication to living out these values in both big ways and small. While at times you may find yourself slipping into old patterns and reacting, I trust that your awareness to course correct will always win! You have this! You are prepared. Just like a best friend whom we love, there is no need for neediness or doubt. Just a willingness to always be there. Remember, you are your very own resilience activator! Everything comes from within.

This joy and heartfelt appreciation are your gift from God.

Receive it and move forward, with love.

JEAN COBINE

Jean Cobine is The Resilience Activator.

After 20+ years in the corporate world working with number crunchers, alongside raising beautiful, strong, resilient daughters, Jean and her Lover (in preference to husband), relocated from New Zealand to living in the warm winter climate on the Gold Coast, Australia. The move was an exciting adventure and an opportunity to re-evaluate 'what's next?'

Looking back, Jean experienced several burnouts in varying chapters of her life with each time presenting another layer of learning.

Most recently in a job for 8.5 years, the volume of work plus an expectant attitude to accept and 'just do it' increased every year, she felt a sense of self-importance, validated from others. Feeling like wonder woman (martyrdom, masculine energy), Jean reached a point where the 'burnout' peaked, coming into full appreciation that the self-importance came at the cost of what's important, her well-being and family.

Jean had forgotten who she was at the core. Jean learnt that she had to put herself first, she had to find the validation from within before she could take the best of her to the roles she played rather than the roles getting the best of her. It was time for massive change! It was time to look within and seek her own self-validation, self-appreciation, and self-worth and it started with getting curious, 'who am I if I'm not this job?' and 'who am I if I'm not the role I play?'

Jean stands for women trusting, belonging in, and fully expressing their authentic selves so they can manifest the life they truly desire with a soft heart and strong spine!

Connect with Jean at heartcentredelevation@gmail.com.

Authentic Self

Jessica Benton

"To thine own self be true," is a famous line from Shakespeare's ***Hamlet***. Its meaning is simple, though not easy: honor who you are in your heart and behave with honesty, integrity, transparency, and authenticity in all.

Simple, but not easy.

Each of us wears many hats: parent, child, sibling, in-law, employee, employer, mentor, mentee, community member, volunteer, significant other, friend, ally, advocate – the list is innumerable – and with each hat, a different aspect of who we are steps into the light, suppressing the others so that it may shine.

The same is true when we find ourselves entangled with the eternal battle of the mind and the heart. To which are we to give greater agency, and what are the consequences that follow? Is the risk worth the possible reward? With two pathways, both winding and uncertain, how do you discern which is the correct path for you? Oftentimes, major decisions don't allow the option to follow both paths.

Recently, I faced this very challenge. In May, my father-in-law became terribly ill. I felt called to support my family: mother-in-law, brother-in-law, and husband (the heart), and still I had the very real responsibility of fulfilling my obligations to my employer (the mind). My husband worked from home, so he moved over three hours south to stay with his mother and to be closer to his father and brother. I remained in our home, committed to meeting my work demands. Bills needed paying, so this was the responsible thing to do. When I wasn't working, I was traveling south to support my family to the best of my ability, then returning home. My schedule was four days of work, drive, two and a half days south, drive.

Rinse. Repeat.

This routine continued for eight weeks. During that time, I watched from afar, alone, as the health of the man I knew as MY dad for almost 30 years slowly deteriorated. Never having a father of my own, he filled a void that I had long forgotten. He joked, told stories, played games, taught me how to shoot clay pigeons, shared his adventures as a tour guide (post-retirement gig), listened with compassion and gave advice. Whenever we'd visit, you'd find the pair of us watching baseball or football on the TV while the rest of the family made themselves scarce. I loved him as if he were my flesh and blood.

Becoming exhausted meant simply that this arrangement wasn't sustainable anymore. I knew my work was suffering. The text updates, the worrying and overthinking about it all was consuming. I was alone and exhausted: mentally, physically, and emotionally. The longer I was away from his side, the more resentment I felt. Yet, I am an adult. Adults' emotions aren't supposed to rule them. They put their adult pants on and face the day, regardless of the heartache felt, because that's what adults **DO**.

I've never been one to set boundaries, especially for my well-being. It's been a life-long process to move me up the proverbial list of what's important. Prior to take-off, the flight attendant instructs the passengers to put on their oxygen mask first so that they may be able to help others. I would be the foolish one running up and down the aisle covering everyone else's face until I collapsed, unconscious. I rarely place my needs above others; I'm working on that.

A mentor shared with me during one of our monthly meetings that to achieve fulfillment, it is crucial to identify what matters most, what aligns with your personal mission, vision, and values, and to set boundaries that honor your authenticity. It was something I knew, and even shared as advice to dozens of people over the years. I simply never considered taking my own wisdom to heart.

In early July, I had a meeting with leadership at my organization. I knew, despite a very uncertain future, there was only one option for me. To remain loyal to my value system, I couldn't sustain working AND caregiving.

I took a leap of faith and chose my heart.

It was then, without consulting anyone, I made the decision to retire early. Yes, there would be penalties for doing so, but that was immaterial. What was important was being with my family during their time of need.

I have never left a job without having a backup plan. I served this organization loyally for 21 years. This was my metaphorical jumping off a cliff and trusting that I would spread wings and fly. I trusted my intuition, despite not knowing what the future would hold.

And, after announcing my retirement, all I felt was relief. I knew where I belonged, and it wasn't at my work desk.

Simple, not easy.

My father-in-law spent his last four months in two different hospitals, a wound-care facility, and, finally, hospice. Because of my choice, I was able to spend the last six weeks with him and the rest of my family, providing comfort to him, and support for the others. I learned about his condition, and when he was cognizant, I listened to many stories of his childhood I had never known.

The strengthening of our family bond far exceeded what money could provide. My choice, my decision, was worth the consequence and I regretted nothing.

The Universe (or whatever spiritual belief system you subscribe to), has a way of taking care of us if we just believe. After the funeral in September, and an appropriate amount of time to grieve the loss of a tremendous man, I started earnestly seeking those new adventures and new opportunities. I knew I had skills, experiences, and gifts that were transferable, if only a hiring team would give me a chance to prove it.

And, with all my trust that things would work out in the end, I will be honest, my belief in myself and the Universe waivered. First, I applied to jobs that I knew would align with my personal values: compassion, honesty, integrity, dignity, grace, and uplifting others. Daily, I'd send out dozens of job applications; first locally, then statewide, and finally to remote positions where I could work from home. And day after day came emails telling me – reinforcing to me – that I wasn't good enough. "*Thank you for your application. The pool was extremely talented. Unfortunately, we've chosen to move forward with other candidates.*" This became my curse. How do you remain confident - courageous - when it feels like you're the only one in the world that believes you'd be an asset to any organization?

It was horrible. I was trapped in a "Groundhog Day" loop; a never-ending cycle of excitement and disappointment. I hunted my Questing Beast while organizations I applied to pursued their Unicorn. The odds seemed astronomically against me. I withdrew from family and friends, my support. As someone with a lifelong history of depression and anxiety, all this rejection fed into my inner demons. I wasn't as talented as I thought I was. Doubt is a terrible companion. I would retreat to paint, write, watch bad serials on TV, or sleep after a day's slog through potential job opportunities. I mean, if a company couldn't see my potential as a Manager Trainee for a convenience store, what more could I do? Thoughts of flipping burgers or becoming a barista just to pay the bills overwhelmed me. Deep down, I knew I had more to give.

I *wanted* to give more. *I longed for purpose in my life.* Where was the Universe when I needed it most?

Then one day, an old friend and colleague sent me a link for a job on a social media site we both belonged to with the message, "I promise, you'll never have to take minutes again." That, honestly, was a HUGE selling point. I opened the description and found that I met most of the requirements. But as study after study has reported, women are less likely to apply for positions where they don't meet a high threshold of what a job expects. Still, it was an opportunity. It *was in higher education*, which I desperately missed; but at a flagship university and in a department *I knew nothing about*. To not apply was the only guarantee to not getting the position.

So, I did.

Weeks passed and I heard nothing. This had become a daily scenario; I'd apply, then… Then the call for the interview came. First there was elation, quickly followed by panic. How was I going to convince this amazing organization, in the capital city, that I was exactly what they needed? The Zoom interview came and, before I knew it, it was over. The next day, they contacted me for a second interview. For Friday. Forty-eight hours after the initial interview. *What?! Is this really happening?!* Again, my heart soared at the possibility; but I'd have to impress department heads that I would fill the void in their team. They were looking for someone with my skillset who also had a passion for diversity and inclusion. This was a dream opportunity. I'd be lying if I said the thought of impressing the final decision makers didn't take the wind out of my sails. So, I prepared, spending hours reviewing the university, the department, and the job description. I knew I needed to nail it. Once more, the Zoom interview took place. It felt good (I usually feel good after an interview only to have someone else be more qualified).

That was the longest weekend **ever**.

Monday, the job offer came. They wanted me, *for me.* My authenticity showed through, despite not answering the scenario questions 100% correct. They saw my value. My worth. *My potential.* No longer did I feel like an imposter, aimlessly trying to convince the world that I had something to contribute. I found my professional home. I graciously accepted the offer. There *may* have been an extended "happy dance" with a few whoops of excitement after I ended the call. Only my husband could confirm, and he's sworn to secrecy.

Now, to the logistics – selling our home and moving three hours south. Uprooting our family and leaving the home that I raised my son in would be emotional. It was truly a time of new beginnings: a new career, a new city to call home, *a new me.*

The Universe never doubted, even when my faith faltered.

"To thine own self be true." It takes tremendous courage, strength, and integrity to remain authentic despite the consequences. It's so much easier to accept something less than your value and your worth. It is a choice – *a mindset* – to remain true to your purpose, regardless of the overwhelming odds. It's more than possessing a positive mental attitude (though, that helps as like attracts like); it's about committing fully to yourself in a way that it becomes your life's mission. By owning your authenticity and allowing it to be your life compass, you will discover magical opportunities (whether you win or you learn) as you navigate life.

JESSICA BENTON

Jessica Benton is a 21-year veteran of higher education. Putting herself through college, she's earned a BS: Political Science & International Studies, an MS: Management and a Diversity & Inclusion advanced certificate. She believes in life-long learning and that personal/professional growth doesn't happen in a vacuum.

Her hobbies include reading, writing, fantasy shopping, painting, role-playing, playing games, and spending time with her family. When she isn't fantasizing about how to drive her husband wacky, she escapes to Netflix, Amazon Prime & Disney+.

Jess is purpose-driven and enthusiastic about removing barriers that prevent people from achieving their dreams and in eliminating inequity gaps for underrepresented, under-served, marginalized/minoritized populations. Her dream is to create a Positive Revolution, drawing on her sphere of like-minded colleagues to come together to create sustainable, positive, socio-economic, and political impact for future generations.

Currently, she volunteers on two inclusion committees serving north central Wisconsin and is a member of Toastmasters International #782. She lives with her husband in Wausau, Wisconsin.

Connect with Jess at

https://www.linkedin.com/in/jessica-benton-msm/.

In the Eye of the Crocodile: Lessons from the World's Toughest Race

Kathy Reesor Oevering

I was canoeing down a river in the Australian outback in the dead of night. It was very quiet except the sound of our paddles splashing in the water, and very dark except for the faraway stars and the beams of our headlamps on the black water. Then, as I looked to the side, I noticed red twinkles lining the shoreline: freshwater crocodiles. They eye gleamed on both sides as we travelled past. There was nowhere to go except straight ahead.

I was always a sporty girl. Shy, but I loved sports. They became my identity and my source of confidence. I excelled as an amateur endurance athlete in running, mountain biking and triathlons. But I was ready for new challenge. I have no idea why I love the sports I do, but I just do. I couldn't explain why, but my own instincts were telling me that something needed to change and what my next challenge would be.

After carefully weighing my options, I chose to go *way* out of my comfort zone. I would do something that I thought only "other" people do, not people like me. I got selected to be on a team to do the Eco-Challenge Adventure Race – an intensely challenging, multi-day event developed by Mark Burnett before he created Survivor. It was to be internationally televised on Discovery Channel, and now years later, the event has been re-vamped and is now called the "World's Toughest Race." There were teams selected from around the world and each had to have one male and one female – so most were three guys and one gal. Besides me, the team was made up of one former military, one mountaineer/climber and one kayak guide – all with some great base of fitness.

It was to be a six-to-ten-day race where each team would decide how much or little to sleep each day. There were certain time cutoffs that you had to make. The sports involved were hiking – not always on a trail – with topographical maps and good 'ol compass, mountain biking, horseback riding, canoeing, rappelling, ascending (the opposite of rappelling), kayaking and whitewater rafting. All this took place in the Australian outback and along its northeast coast amongst wild kangaroos, wild pigs, venomous snakes and spiders, crocodiles, and ocean creatures; plus, stinging nettles and other hazardous plants you had to be careful of.

The intensity of the race situation and the height of emotions surrounding it, have etched vivid detail into my mind so that I can recall parts of the vent clearly even years later. It would become a significant highlight of my life, something that shaped the woman I became and was meant to be. I also go to explore where my own limits physically, mentally, emotionally, and spiritually were – the good, the bad and the ugly.

I spent most of my extra time the next several months training, planning, taking courses and certifications so make sure we met all the required skills to be tested before the race. It was intense, but I loved it – most of it.

Up to this point, I used to have to workout really hard, I mean *really* hard regularly, or I was super bitchy. If I kept working out *really* hard,

I was fun and happy. With spending so much time with my teammates and not always working out, the intensity of the situation in training somehow were bringing all the years of stuffed-down emotions to the surface. It was just an intense mix of so many that all I knew was that I didn't think clearly all the time, did things that didn't make sense and was overly reactive to things that wasn't my normal nature. *What was happening to me?* I wondered.

On top of this, for the first time in my life at that point, someone very close to me passed very suddenly, so was feeling deep grief on top of everything else. But with less than two months before the race, I didn't have the time or energy to deal with this properly. It did make for some team struggles and didn't help us gel together as well as we might have. It was only later that I learned how team unity is a key element required to be really successful.

About a month before the race, I wanted to quit. I was frustrated by my emotional turmoil; the training wasn't fun anymore and I wanted to get to the bottom of it. I felt like I wasn't going to be friends with my teammates after the race and, if I quit now, I could at least have a fun summer with my other friends. I loved and cherished the adventure of all the training, so felt like I had already grown and challenged myself. But I had *committed* to myself and my teammates and spent a lot of time and money to get this far. I didn't want to let my teammates down as they would have been hard-pressed to replace me at that late stage. Plus, a cool adventure was waiting for me down in Australia. So, bravely I kept moving forward.

We arrived in the Land Down Under with so much excitement for this huge event and meet the other racers from all over the world. We had a whole week's worth of meeting, skill testing, gear checks and fun events. We got to meet Mark Burnett himself. We had not one but *two* meetings about all the wild plants and animals that we needed to be aware of. We had to balance all of this activity with making sure we were rested for the biggest race of our lives.

Finally, the night before the race start, we got our maps, list of checkpoints and the chance to plot out our route and organize our gear for each of the sports. There was some mandatory gear we had to carry with us at all times and some specific gear for each sport depending on the leg of the journey. Food was up to us. Water was from wherever we could find it and drop in a foul-tasting iodine tablet to purify it. There were three major checkpoints/camps during the race where we could restock our food, change out gear and they would supply us with a hot meal, toilets, and a cot to sleep on – basically heaven in the middle of an adventure race.

The next day we headed straight inland from the coast on a bus for about four hours into the Australian outback. We sat around for a couple of hours in the hot sun, and just to test us further, we were to start the race at dusk.

Finally, as we all stood eager and ready at the start line, the most venomous snake in the world slithered across our path – the inland Taipan!!! Race start was delayed. *Holy Crap!!*

So, what do I do? Willingly hike into the outback knowing that these snakes are out there, knowing that I'll be sleeping on a tarp with no real protections from any critter out there? Do I turn back and quit? Do I let my teammates down after all this time?! Nope – I dug deep and embraced my courage just to start this damn thing. No one else quit either.

After a couple of days of hiking, canoeing in the dark with the crocodiles, and a run in with a wild boar, my feet were getting seriously blistered, and I was starting to get tired. We had already done a couple of ropes sections of repelling, ascending and a tyrolean traverse (like a zip line), when we came to the last and most challenging ropes section.

Rope work was one of the disciplines that I didn't have much experience in prior to the race. I had to clip, unclip, clip, repeat over and over while hiking over big rocks, and not feeling great. I stopped for a minute – behind enough so my teammates couldn't see me – and let out a big, sobbing cry. I was so tired and frustrated, but I didn't want my teammates to see that I was "weak" especially when we weren't getting along all the time anyway. Once we regrouped, I kept looking up at this huge cliff that went straight up, trying not to cry. My teammates thought I was super scared and reassured that it would be all right. I didn't tell them that I wasn't scared or the real reason.

The next part of the ascent was an overhand so your feet are dangling in the air in footloops and couldn't touch any rock. This was trickier than the previous ascent where you touch the rock, but once your gear was setup and you were only your way – you couldn't change it up. I was going nowhere fast with how my gear was set up and wanted to cry out of sheer frustration and emotional and physical exhaustion. My teammates, of course, whipped up to the top like pro-climbers. I was stuck in the middle. I am not one to give up easily, but I asked what would happen if I did. A three-hour penalty.

I didn't want to let my team down, so I calmed myself, took a deep breath and just slowly made my way up that big cliff. Finally, I got to the top and my team gave a big cheer!!! The next section was the first mountain bike leg which was my strongest sport!! I was never so happy to get on my bike and feel confident again.

After nine days from the start of the race, many blisters, breaking a toe when my horse stepped on my foot, ocean storms while kayaking and a minor medical issue later – *we finished the race!!* Of the forty-nine teams that started, only twenty-nine finished – and we were twenty fourth!! I was elated and had reached my goal! I was ready for a good rest, a long hot shower and downtime to figure out that to do with my emotional state.

Three months later, the race was televised in segments, for five days in a row. I watched every minute of it. Only then, did I realize that we had no idea what was happening outside of our own team's experience! On TV, we saw the struggles the other teams went through, and some were *way* more experienced than us; the injuries, the setback, team fighting worse than our, but also their great moments and celebrations along the way. I felt grateful and proud that I had.

That cryfest I had on the ropes. I watched a segment when one of the toughest gals I had seen before the race, also cried a couple of times during the race, just like me. Maybe I wasn't bad after all. It showed profoundly how we never know what's going on for others. I cried every episode. I hadn't realized how much tension was there to let go of and I was starting to feel "good enough" inside again.

Now, I recognize that almost all of you reading this will never want to do what I did. But what do you want to do? Do you just have an urge that something needs to change? Do you just need to add more intensity and passion to whatever you are already doing? Some may take easy action on these things. Others may feel resistant and blocked. If this story has helped inspire you to take action for yourself, then telling this story has served its purpose.

Live your best day!!

KATHY REESOR OEVERING

Kathy has been sporty her whole life, was a former varsity runner, and then turned to triathlons. She became a Nationally Ranked Triathlete, Provincial Champion, Top 5 International in Age Group for Olympic Distance, and has completed Ironman twice. With her love of the outdoors, she competed in adventure racing starting with Mark Burnett's Internationally televised Ecochallenge, now known as the World's Toughest Race!!

Since then, she has done many backpacking and kayaking trips, mountain climbing (including falling in a big crevasse and lived to tell the tale), and rock climbing. She has helped coach in triathlons and running as well as coaching her kids in Cross-country skiing.

Kathy intimately knows the importance of being healthy and keeping injury free as part of her success. Kathy has an extensive background in healthcare as a physical therapist and osteopath, with both traditional training and too many holistic modalities to list. Her strength is blending the traditional with holistic modalities to treat the whole person.

Whether coaching in the healthcare setting, sports, or life/performance/sales coaching, she loves to inspire others to live more passionately and authentically. You do not have to be an athlete to work with Kathy as she has had the patience to help her mother with lots of tech. She is also an international speaker. When Kathy isn't doing this, she and her husband happily run after her twin girls.

If you are feeling stuck and would like some help from someone who has been there to take whatever new action is right for you, you can learn more about Kathy and her story at www.kathyreesor.com.

Taking a Leap of Faith~Finding the Courage to Listen to My Intuition

Kathy Shelor

My legs ached and I could not stand on them. They would not support my weight. I was twenty years old, in my second year of college at Arizona State University and I was lying in a hospital bed with bright red blotches covering my legs. Doctor after doctor came in examining me and my legs and said, "I don't know what that is" as they looked at my legs. I was so surprised; how could they not know what was happening to me?

My mom stood faithfully by my hospital bed listening to each doctor. Friends came to see me bringing cards and stuffed animals, but I didn't have the energy to visit with them. I was scared. I felt sick to my stomach and unsure as I looked at the IV tube connected to my arm. What was happening to me? How did I end up here? Why was my body acting like this? I finally fell asleep, thankful to have my mom's calm presence and love by my side.

The next morning, the red spots and blotches had worsened on my legs and now they were spreading up into my stomach. My joints ached and were swollen. Another doctor came in and observed my condition, he didn't really say anything, and left. Finally, at ten in the morning, a dermatologist walked into my hospital room. She examined me and she said, "I know exactly what this is." I couldn't believe it, I felt such relief, finally somebody who knew what was wrong with me. "You have allergic vasculitis" and I said, "What is that?" "It is when your body is having an extreme allergic reaction to a drug, or an infection and it is causing your blood vessels to pop under your skin. The red spots and blotches are actually blood under your skin. If it goes untreated, you could die." Fortunately, the doctor put me on a high dose of prednisone, which stopped my immune system from attacking my blood vessels. They discharged me from the hospital with strict orders. I had to limit my walking and keep my feet elevated as much as possible for the next two months. I remember thinking, Wow, without modern medicine I could've died. If I had lived one hundred years ago, I would not have survived. This was a good wake up call for me. It started me thinking about my life. What if I only had a brief time to live, what would I do with it?

I reflected on my life, I finally was an adult, and I could really go anywhere, and do anything. My first year of college had been great sharing a dorm room with my best friend. I had enjoyed living away from home and becoming an independent adult. I liked biking to my classes under the palm trees in the warm Arizona sun and meeting new friends from all over the United States. My second year of college had been different. The kids were not serious about studying, a lot of them were more interested in partying and my classes were so big. My economics class was in an auditorium and had almost five hundred people in it. I could barely understand my statistics teacher due to his heavy accent, is this higher education? I wanted smaller classes and to be around people who were interested in their learning. I knew I needed a more academic atmosphere. I wanted more enthusiastic instructors and a new, inspiring place to live. I could have died; I want to live my life and do something with it! So, where could I go? I wanted to go somewhere new and different. After talking to various people, I finally decided I wanted to go to the east coast and experience college life there. I wanted to go to an exciting city like Boston, New York City or

Washington DC, because there was no internet (this was 1989), I started writing to schools for information about their programs. I ended up applying to colleges on the east coast as I finished my second year of college at ASU, while keeping my legs elevated as much as possible.

Over the summer, I received an acceptance letter from New York University (NYU). I was interested and excited about the possibility, so my mom, dad and I took a trip to New York City. We had never been to New York before and the very busyness of it was exciting, but also overwhelming. My dad hated it, and he did not feel safe. It was loud and dirty and there was so much energy and movement. When we got to NYU in Greenwich Village, I found it more appealing, because you don't have the giant skyscrapers towering over you, making you feel so small. This area of New York City was more low-key, and I loved how pretty the brownstone houses and trees were bordering the very urban Washington Square Park. We took a school tour, but I wasn't sure if I should go to school there? I liked the school, but New York City scared me. We went home and I was undecided.

As I thought about where to go to college, a strong feeling in the pit of my stomach told me to go to NYU. I couldn't explain it, and I tried to ignore it, but I kept getting a feeling that I should go there. I didn't really want to go, but this feeling would not leave me. Finally, I decided to embrace courage and take a leap and I said, "Yes, I will try it." In my mind, I told myself, I can always go back to ASU if this doesn't work out. My dad and brothers were against my decision to go to NYU. My only supporter was my mother, who encouraged me and said, "I think it will be good for you." Thank goodness for her love, openness, and support.

So, in the fall of 1989, I started my third year of college in an apartment style dormitory mostly with transfer students in their third year of college. NYU did an excellent job matching us up. We were six girls, most of them were second generation Americans from various parts of the US or the world. I had a French roommate, an Italian roommate, a Greek roommate, and even a Peruvian roommate! How fun, to meet young college students from distinct parts of the world and the best part of all we were all serious about learning. Nobody was there to party. I was still scared of walking the streets alone. Remember, this was NYC in the late 1980s, the city was raw and gritty. Across the street from where I lived, there was a crack house. They sold drugs on the corner, and prostitutes gathered on another corner. Slowly, I adapted and got use to things. I was having fun meeting so many interesting people with so many innovative ideas. I was enjoying my classes and I had good teachers. Life and learning had become exciting again. The weather started changing. The fall colors appeared, and I grew used to my new surroundings. I soon began to like my new life in NYC. It was so vibrant and so different from my life in sunny, dry Arizona. Just imagine if I hadn't listened to my intuition and embraced courage, I would have stayed in Arizona and not grown as much. I ended up living in NYC for seven years. I grew so much as a person. I met so many interesting people from around the world, learned about diverse cultures, religions and I learned about art.

Now, fast forward into 2014, I am living in San Diego. I am married and a mother to two boys ages six and eight. It is back to school night at our local elementary school. There is a signup sheet for volunteers to help in the classroom. Most of the volunteer spots are full. I see they need a volunteer to teach art once a month. A brief moment of interest and excitement blooms in my stomach. Then fear comes in, how could I teach an art class? I'm not a teacher. I find a chair and sit down and listen to my son's teacher explain what she is going to teach the kids throughout the year. My mind drifts over to the volunteer sheet. I'd like to volunteer, and be in the classroom a little bit, but I'm not a teacher. I don't like standing up in front of people. I'm scared to teach. What if I make a mistake? I dismiss the thought of teaching, but there's that feeling in the pit of my stomach, telling me to sign up. I don't want to sign up. I'm not a teacher. So, I decide to let fate decide. I tell myself, if no one signs up to teach art, then I will do it. I go back to listening to the teacher.

After the teacher finishes talking, I check out the classroom, stalling hoping somebody signs up to be the volunteer art teacher. As the classroom, empties out, I make my way over to the volunteer sheet, and nobody has signed up to teach art. My stomach gets excited, my mind gets scared, but I write my name down on the sign-up sheet. The teacher comes over to me and thanks me for signing up. She is so happy to have an art volunteer. I tell her I will try and do my best, but still the nagging self-doubt comes in.

Fortunately, the art program is well organized. Each grade level learns about eight different master artists (Van Gogh, Monet) during the school year. There are lesson plans for each month and sample art lessons included. I find I really like learning about the artists and practicing the art lessons at home. I remember, for my first art class, I was so nervous, I wrote out a script and I practiced it several times in front of the mirror. In the classroom, to my surprise, I found the kids listened quietly and were very happy to create art. I found I liked seeing what they created. It took about four or five classes before I finally got over my nervousness. As I start to teach more, I find the kids are always very excited to see me coming in with art supplies. I know what I am doing is worth it, they are learning about famous artists and creating art and I am learning how to be a teacher.

Just imagine, if I hadn't listened to my intuition, embraced courage, and tried teaching, the kids would not have had any art that year and I would still be scared to speak in front of a class. I continued to teach art lessons each year for both my boys while they were in elementary school. After my first year of teaching, I ended up being in charge of the whole art volunteer program. Once again, I embraced courage and took on the role. In the process, I learned how to coordinate volunteers, communicate well, and share my love of art with elementary aged kids and parent volunteers.

In 2019, I turned fifty and I found myself a little surprised at how fast the time has gone by in my life. This milestone got me thinking, what do I want to accomplish in the next twenty years of my life? What can I contribute to the world? How can I make the world a happier, more peaceful place? I recently taught a workshop called, "The Joy Laboratory," where we brainstormed the idea, "What brings us Joy?" For the next twenty-one days, we all did one joyful activity a day and we thought of three things for which we were thankful. At the end of the twenty-one days, I noticed I felt lighter, happier, and more appreciative of life. I had great feedback from the participants, too, about how they are finding joy in everyday life and appreciating life more. After the Covid-19 pandemic and with all the unrest in the world, I feel drawn to making the world a happier, more peaceful place. A new pathway is emerging for me of painting, teaching, and joyful living. I am listening to my intuition, embracing courage, and saying "Yes" to life!

Looking back over my life, I realize how important it is to embrace courage, even if you're scared. You don't know what you will learn or how you will grow unless you try. So, the next time, you want to try something new, but you are scared, say "let me try." Let's embrace courage and see what happens.

KATHY SHELOR

Kathy Shelor is an artist, a holistic health practitioner, and a transformational life coach with a business and accounting background. She enjoys sharing her energy and enthusiasm for life with others by leading small workshops on joyful living and by creating art. She lives in California with her husband, two teenage boys, three cats, and "Goldie" her golden retriever dog.

Connect with Kathy at www.kathyshelor.com.

Turning Fear into Courage

Lynda Sunshine West

When I was 5 years old, I ran away from home and was gone for an entire week. I only went to the next-door neighbor's house so I was safe. I'm sure the neighbor called my mom and told her I was there, but she let me stay. After a week, my mom called the neighbor and told her it was time for me to come home, "Lynda's been gone long enough. You can send her home now."

That week became instrumental in my belief system. Nobody came to get me and I created within my own mind a firm belief that no one wanted me around and nobody loved me. At five years old, this belief was locked in tight, and I would hold onto that belief the next 46 years.

As you might imagine, I was growing up in an abusive home. When I came home, I became riddled with fear and, as a result, became the ultimate people-pleaser. Whenever people asked me to do anything, I would say "YES" because I was afraid they wouldn't like me if I said "NO."

High school became a petri dish for fear. While I was saying yes to my friends, I was also lashing out at other students. My efforts to please one group (my "friends") caused me to be mean to others. Even my friends made fun of me. To compensate, I started making fun of myself. And I was good at it, too. I became my own worst enemy.

This behavior of being mean to myself and allowing others to be mean to me didn't get any better after high school.

Right out of high school I married someone just like my dad. I didn't recognize it as an abusive relationship because it was just a continuation of how I had grown up. My first husband yelled at me on a daily basis, "You're so stupid. You're so ignorant. People only like you because they feel sorry for you." The worst part is that I believed him.

I ended the marriage after two years and two babies. I decided one day that I'm was going to stay in an abusive relationship like my mom did, so I walked out the door with a diaper bag over one shoulder, my purse over the other, one child (14 months old) on my hip, and one child (4 weeks old) in her baby carrying case. That may sound like a brave thing to do, but I did it because my fear of staying was stronger than my fear of leaving.

My work life had its own set of issues. I moved from job to job to job (49 of them in 36 years). I always felt underappreciated, so I quit to find someone who would appreciate me and my abilities. I came up with new ideas and my bosses wouldn't listen to them. I was afraid of saying the wrong thing and people thinking I was stupid. And whenever I did something "good," people called me a brown-noser.

So I started to shut down and stopped using my voice. "Was it because I was stupid like my ex-husband said I was? Could he have been right?" is what I thought.

Fast forward to August of 2014. I was driving to my 49th job working for a judge in the Ninth Circuit Court of Appeals, sitting in traffic (like I had been doing for many decades). As I was stuck in that traffic, an overwhelming sense of dread, disgust, and anger engulfed my body. Here I was, 51 years old, pounding on the steering wheel and saying, "What is this all about, what is this planet all about, why are we here, why do we have to do this, what is my life all about, literally '**why am I here?**'"

When I got to work there was a post in a Facebook group that said, "I'm a life coach. I took some time off and I'm getting back into it. I'm looking for five women who want to change their life." She was talking directly to me. I hired her and we worked together the next five months.

The most instrumental exercise we did together helped me see myself through the eyes of others (positive people only), which, in turn, helped me transform from my own worst enemy into my own best cheerleader.

When our contract was up, I was on my own, all alone, no more help. I had the tools she supplied me with to keep growing, but I wanted more growth and I wanted it NOW! I had gotten so accustomed to changing and growing that I had become addicted to positivity. That positivity had slowed down because my life coach was no longer with me.

Something snapped inside of me when I woke up on January 1, 2015. Something was different. I had an epiphany and said to myself, "I have so many fears that are stopping me from living my life. I'm going to break through one fear every day this year." So I did.

Every morning for 365 days I would wake up. Before getting out of bed, I would ask myself one simple question, three simple words that would change the trajectory of my life: "What scares me?" Then I would wait for the answer to come (sometimes it was immediate and sometimes 10 minutes).

I started by facing agonizing fears like talking to strangers, starting a conversation, and going to networking events. Little fears to some people, but huge fears to me.

About three months into the fear busting journey, I was brushing my teeth and reciting an acronym I had heard many times before: False Evidence Appearing Real. False Evidence Appearing Real. Staring at myself, I realized that acronym is a lie.

I broke it down and realized that there was nothing false about my fear. My fears are as real as can be to me. There was no evidence of anything. They didn't appear real; They were real.

I came to the conclusion that when I tapped into my faith, it was much easier for me to break through my fears. You can't have faith and fear at the same time; they are opposites. I also realized that fear is nothing more than anxiety or nervousness and came up with my own acronym: Faith Erases Anxious Reactions. When your faith is strong, your fear is weak. You just need to tap into your faith: faith in yourself, faith in others, and faith in God.

Over the next 90 days, I conquered fears such as asking someone to do something for me, speaking on stage, asking a celebrity to endorse my book.

After 180 days of fears, I looked back on the previous six months and asked myself a question, "What's the common theme between these fears? There's gotta be something." That's when I had another epiphany - the majority of my fears were caused by the fear of judgment.

Something as simple as starting a conversation with a stranger can be difficult for many of us. In my case, it was the fear of saying something stupid or ignorant.

Armed with this knowledge, I was able to tackle the next six months with a mission to rid myself of the fear of judgment. By the end of the year, judgment was no longer an issue for me. I did it. I tackled and conquered it.

While I was ridding myself of the fear of judgment, I came up with a simple 7-step process to help me quickly and easily break through fear EVERY TIME and I'm going to share it with you here. Take out a pen and paper and take notes. This may change your life exponentially.

The first thing is to identify a fear you want to overcome. Write it down. Maybe you're a rockstar at work and know you're underpaid, but you're afraid of asking for a raise; maybe you have a great idea or passion to start a new business but the idea of starting it paralyzes you; maybe you want to write a book, but the thought of putting your story on paper scares you. I have experienced ALL of these in the past, and, yes, they're all connected to the fear of judgment.

To demonstrate my simple 7-step process, let's use writing a book as the fear we're going to tackle. This was one of my greatest fears, the one where my knees were shaking, my throat locked up, my palms were sweaty, and my memory escaped me once I started writing.

In the scenario of writing a book, the first question you ask yourself is …

"If I write a book [insert your fear here], will it adversely affect my life one year from today?"

The first component of this sentence is to clearly state your fear.

Then we come to the word "Adversely." Why that word? If you leave out the word "adversely," you're left with "will it affect my life." Yes, it can affect your life in a positive or negative way. By adding the word "adversely," you're asking if doing this action will affect your life in a bad way.

Then we have the words, "one year." I start here because the majority of fears will not adversely affect your life one year from today. In the case of writing a book, the worst thing that may happen is you are critiqued by someone who doesn't like your book. But a year from now, you may not even remember that critique happened. Time has a way of putting things into perspective. Seeing a situation with this timeframe puts you into a realistic state of mind and that is necessary in order to quickly and easily break through fears.

Finally, we have the words “from today.” I was breaking through one fear every single day for a year, so it was important that I break through that fear <u>that day</u>. Waiting until tomorrow I would then have two fears to break through. This ended up being a brilliant idea because it forced me to exercise my fear breaking muscle. Breaking through fears became easier and easier because fear became part of my comfort zone. I ENLARGED the size of my comfort zone.

The second step is asking the same full question, but this time changing only the timeframe.

“If I <u>write a book</u> [<u>insert your fear here</u>], will it adversely affect my life **six months** from today?”

Like the one-year timeframe, there is still no downside in six months.

Now change six months to one month, then change one month to one week, and next change one week to one day.

Here’s where it gets a little funky. Depending on the fear you’re facing, one week from breaking through the fear you may still feel a little queasy inside. You may still feel the effects of breaking through that fear. This is because you’ve moved back into an emotional state of mind, even though, logically, you know you’re okay. Let’s say you responded that writing a book will NOT adversely affect your life one week from today.

As you might have guessed, the next steps are to shorten the timeframe. Let’s go for even shorter.

“If I <u>write a book</u> [<u>insert your fear here</u>], will it adversely affect my life one hour from now?”

And FINALLY....

“If I <u>write a book</u> [<u>insert your fear here</u>], will it adversely affect my life RIGHT NOW?”

You might be wondering why I use seven steps instead of just one. Well, I found that by slowly stepping myself down through each time period, it moved me into a more relaxed state of mind and my logical brain had time to process what I was doing. I was able to more logically answer the questions and not allow my emotions to take over logic and reality.

But what if the answer to the question is YES?

What I have found is that after you break through a fear, you rarely have long-term adverse effects. In those cases where an adverse outcome is "possible," you need to come up with a plan of how to address that. You don't just give up and walk away; you simply recognize that additional work needs to be done to overcome that fear.

If you're afraid of asking for a raise, your plan may be to rehearse what you are going to say to your boss and have an outline of WHY you deserve the raise.

If you're afraid of starting a new business, you may find a mentor who is successfully doing what you want to do and have them guide you so you gain confidence in starting your business.

If you're afraid of writing a book, you may start off with writing just one chapter, like in this collaboration book.

If you're afraid of meeting new people, your plan may be to psyche yourself up before talking to them. I use a word that moves me into a state of confidence and laughter, which also calms my nerves. My word is "SHAZAM!!" What will be your word?

I may not have the same fears as you, but our fears are very real … to each of us. Let's decide right here right now not to allow anyone to rob us of our experience of that fear by telling us it's insignificant or ridiculous.

YOU have the power to break through that fear in that moment, but only you can make that decision. And it has to be a decision that you made FOR YOU.

Yes, fear is scary. But it doesn't have to control your life. In fact, it can make your life better. So when you've identified a fear in your life, face it head on and do it BECAUSE you're scared.

LYNDA SUNSHINE WEST

She ran away at 5 years old and was gone an entire week. She came home riddled with fears and, in turn, became a people-pleaser.

At age 51, she decided to face one fear every day for an entire year. In doing so, she gained an exorbitant amount of confidence and now uses what she learned to fulfill her mission of empowering 5 million women and men to share their stories with the world to make a greater impact on the planet.

Lynda Sunshine West is the Founder and CEO of Action Takers Publishing, a Speaker, 17 Times #1 International Bestselling and Award-Winning Author, Executive Film Producer, and Red Carpet Interviewer.

Connect with Lynda Sunshine at

https://www.actiontakerspublishing.com.

Growing Through the Changes

Niki Hall

I've heard it said so many times. Life doesn't sit still. It's either moving in the direction of living or it's growing in the direction of death. You are constantly growing in one direction or the other. There is no exception to that rule. So many people sit contently thinking they are doing something but doing something often means growth and growth means moving in a direction. Take a good look at your life. Which direction are you moving toward? Often, growth means change and so many of us would prefer not to change things and continue to live in the status quo. Others, like myself, are constantly on the move. Living the life to an improved degree to the constant best of their ability. To do this, because change comes with challenges, one needs courage.

"You will never do anything in this world without courage.
It is the greatest quality of the mind next to honor."
~Aristotle

There are many types of courage:

- Physical Courage ~ when you face something despite the risk of experiencing bodily harm or death.
- Emotional Courage ~ the willingness to face or share your feelings. This could be the shortest path to true feelings of the heart. It involves a full spectrum of emotions.

- Moral Courage ~ facing up to what one thinks is the right thing. Doing right. Despite the possibility of adverse consequences.
- Spiritual Courage ~ Facing life with dignity and faith. Keeps us moving forward even though the result is unseen but believed or is known that it could exist.
- Intellectual Courage ~ Moving through growth or changes with an open mind, letting go of familiarity, moving into new or unknown territory with a willingness to learn, unlearn, and relearn.
- Social Courage ~ to stay yourself despite challenges, the possibility of exclusion, rejection, and conflict.

The conclusion I came to over the years is that you must come to realize the main vehicle to becoming yourself, to achieving your personal goals, to becoming the person that you are meant to be, is that you must travel through all the types of courage. There is no exception here.

Personal growth doesn't need any big disaster, or you don't have to be coming from a devastating position in life to experience the depths of the gamut of emotions and challenges courage makes you face. I assure you, without disrespect to those who do have to come through horrible positions, the pressure, fear, and courage it takes to grow through the changes one must in life are no different than those with challenging depths. They could still cause paralyzing fear, anxiety to the point of dysfunction or complacency and lack of growth.

Today, we are going to talk about coming from an everyday place and trying to make substantial changes. This takes fortitude. To get to the other side of a goal or to live your life as you see and know you can, you are going to have to travel through all the types of courage mentioned. You will need mental and emotional strength, and perseverance, with various degrees of fearlessness, spirit, or spunk. Things may get to feel relentless or cruel. They may also repeat themselves with all types of variation until you get it right or until you reach your goal.

Exercising courage really is no easy feat. It's not easy to achieve. You may have to push through fear, conflict, adversity, and the loss of one thing to gain the other. The price could be a loved one moving in another direction. Never-the-less, you still must be true to yourself and keep moving forward. These could be big prices to pay. Hard prices!

Once you realize you can cope. That the loss really isn't a loss, just a change in the way it's been. That it's simply something different from what you are accustomed to. The balance you appreciate and like to live your life in becomes a little bit better. It becomes a slightly bigger part of you, your peace of mind and identity. Then it's easy to acknowledge, you feel it was worth it and you keep your vision and your goals in perspective. You keep moving forward with a deeper level of self-respect and pleasure or satisfaction.

While I was learning all of this and moving toward learning to embrace courage, before I could get here, I had to keep growing through the changes which started, for me, at an early age.

As a child, I saw differences in me while comparing myself to other kids. I saw my perspectives weren't quite the same. Nothing big to make me "special" in any way. Different enough from the others for me to notice. Eventually, I had to start standing up for myself as others started noticing as well. Of course, most of us had our turns at defending ourselves. Sometimes childhood and living through our teens could get a little should we say… unsure. None of us escaped that one. I took my differences very seriously and started asking myself important questions. The more I asked myself, the more I knew this small town was not where I was meant to stay. I loved that world, but I knew my choices would continue to separate me from the pack and cause me to move on. Which it did.

This is when all means of courage would come into place, while I was trying to live a life I was meant to live. I had goals, a lot of them. I could see that the life I was meant to live was a comfortable and peaceful one. Now my journey was about how to live that vision, the dream that I knew could exist for me. That life included affluence and prosperity.

After years of experience, self-sacrifice and finally knowing better, I now get to add that my goals were about prosperity, affluence and becoming exactly who I was meant to be. Yes, living the life I was meant to live really couldn't happen until I included and was simultaneously becoming the person I honestly am meant to be. It took me years to add myself to that equation. It really doesn't work otherwise. It's such an integral part of the equation. I'm so glad I realized that. No more going around in circles wondering why I'm not getting anywhere.

Also, to get where I needed to go, I had to admit this lifestyle had money attached to it. That meant I would have to reconcile myself to money. How to live with money and live a good and honorable life. I imagine coming from lower middle class and having a wisdom passed down to me from generations, to survive at that level, someone in my past justified that money and corruption led to disobedience and the list went on and on. This was challenging work for my character to feel and accept that living with more money than I grew up around was perfectly fine, healthy, and expected.

You would think that I would be telling you this in some wonderful logical order, but this is real life. We all grow up in different manners and times that don't provide wisdom on how to get to your destiny in the shortest amount of time or in the most efficient way. I was picking pieces of my life to change as they presented themselves. I imagine it would seem to you that they have no outside logical order. It makes sense to me. They are my order, the order I grew my life in. Everyone's order is unique and individual to their present perspectives and their current goals. While going through all sorts of changes you may hear yourself say, I'm so scattered. Realize you aren't really. You're just dealing with things as it reveals itself in your life or in your pathway to growth and achievement. Again, there is an appearance of being scattered. It isn't. The thing that must change isn't in a sensible spot or position like first or last. It's something embedded in your life. It's been there a while so it may have deep tentacles and varying in character or attributes for example. It's not a mess. It's simply something you don't need anymore. It must go and something new must replace it. That's all.

I had moved away, was developing a respectable career and found my life partner. At this point in my life, it was now all about moving into living a good life. I was looking to start my focus and drive to living a prosperous life. This started a whole new phase of growing through the changes. I started by seeking out the wisdom of a highly respected psychologist and a very dear friend of mine. One day while sitting in his kitchen, over a cup of tea, I asked him "How do I get to a goal that I know I could accomplish but have no knowledge of how to get there?" He told me to read biographies, to find the people that have done what I am looking to do and become acquainted with them. Work with them, do activities with them, become friends with them. Surround yourself with people that are better than you, he said, that have achieved things that you respect and want for yourself. He continued, stop being in the company of people that are complacent and happy with staying right where they are. Stay away from negative people. Also avoid those who govern their lives by outside media and advice. Always listen to your own gut. He suggested reading about the successful people that are where you would like to go. This started me on the path of becoming a life-long learner. I still follow his advice to this day. I always will.

Having decided to live by my own beliefs and by what I knew was right for me, I have come to know my own mind. I've developed my abilities and have also come to appreciate my unique qualities. They have become a strength on which I could depend. Being true to myself has kept me away from compromising myself and continuously living in conflict. A result that stemmed from this is that I now like myself more so than I used to and can easily live with myself and my decisions. I enjoy my own company. This has allowed me to enjoy things alone, appreciate my alone time, and to see the value and appreciate the trivial things in life even if there is no one around to share it with. This has such a wonderful value attached to it.

I am so grateful for all that I've learned, who I am, and that my energy is in a beautiful place. I should say that because I am always so grateful, my energy is constantly at a wonderful place. Which ever direction you choose to look at it from, I now live in constant gratitude and my energy is always at a great level. What it took was learning to embrace courage and to constantly be growing through the changes as I moved into new phases of living.

I still have more goals. Big goals. Now that I don't fear change and have learned to embrace courage, I will continue to expand my knowledge and develop specific comprehension. I will continue to choose a direction that is right for my vision, know I can do it, make my decisions and actions count, and believe my goals, dreams and aspirations are worth all the effort. I know after learning all that I have that I could make my own dreams come true. It's for that reason that I will continue to set goals. Living in a state of clarity that enables me to see If I put my mind to it, it could make it happen. I could achieve that goal. Anybody can!

NIKI HALL

Niki Hall is a Mindset Coach. Realizing her personal ability to help people, she opened a self-help school.

She later authored a book entitled *Building Up - Thoughts Expressed During the Readjustment of Self*, a book on Change and Self-Actualization, where her first printing sold out within days of its release. This catapulted her into public speaking and workshop engagements.

Now, Niki has hung a shingle out to help people break through their limited beliefs and to achieve more prosperity in their health, wealth, or business.

Connect with Niki at https://www.facebook.com/niki.hall.148.

Surviving to Thriving: Embracing Self-Worth Courageously

Rachel Lounds

"Love yourself first and everything else falls into line. You really have to love yourself to get anything done in this world." ~Lucille Ball

Average.

For most of my life, average was the word I would use to describe myself. Plain Jane. Nothing special. Mediocre. Real inspirational, right? I don't really know where this came from, but it has been the theme of my existence for much of my life – average. Ironically, it was when I was in the midst of hitting rock bottom that I discovered I am, in fact, exceptional. That's the frustrating truth of this rollercoaster of life, isn't it? Want to truly feel exceptional? Cool, here's absolute rock bottom; you'll know the contrast when you get to the other side.

The journey to self-love is no different. As a female, I'm sure you understand. Want to love, really, truly, love yourself? Well, it probably starts with some intense self-loathing. Then, one day, enough is enough. It's time to make a change. It's time to climb.

Both my parents were teachers. My father was very ambitious, with clear intentions to become a high school principal. His own damaged childhood meant he placed impossible expectations on himself, later projecting them onto the rest of the family, who could never really measure up.

To receive his love meant I had to be extraordinary, something I knew was impossible for me – my parents often reiterated that I was an average student and definitely not on par with my brother. I failed the eleven-plus exam at the end of primary school and so didn't get into the local grammar school. I refused to go to a private school and board, and this in my father's eyes made me a huge disappointment. Something I carried with me for a very long time.

I was not only average, but a disappointment

Because of this I felt very rejected by my parents and that I had no real place in our family. I was left confused about what it was I was supposed to do, who I was supposed to be and where and I was supposed to go. I honestly didn't have a clue what I wanted to be, and this often played on a loop in my mind, reinforced by my father's voice confirming that I didn't really know what I was doing.

So, I drifted.

I was not what you call a classic drifter, living out of a bag and hand to mouth. As far as drifters go, I was the antithesis. I was settled with a home, a car, a stable job and a wardrobe full of designer clothes. My mind was a whole different story. I felt like much of my life had been a bit of a blur, yes, I'd lived, but had I lived it intentionally? Definitely not.

I went to university because I was told to by my father and my school. I went to London because that's what everyone did after uni. I got a job in advertising because it seemed like something I could probably do. In essence, I was directionless. I didn't know what I wanted because my inner intuitive compass was off, flattened by the expectations of society, highly critical parents, and the education system.

I came to Australia to escape and to 'find myself'. The only thing I found was more of the same life I had been living before. But now, twenty years later, I have finally woken up.

So, what happened?

I lost my job. In December 2019 I was let go from my company after four years of what I would call some of the worst career years of my life. By the time I left, I was a shell of a person. I was suffering from anxiety and insomnia, and I had absolutely no confidence or self-worth.

'We have to let you go.' My rock bottom. My first step. My climb.

It was those five words that catapulted me into the beginning of something amazing and new.

I have always loved helping and seeing other people flourish and grow, and towards the end of my advertising career I had developed an interest in positive psychology. Losing your job is a lonely experience. People suddenly don't want to be your friend anymore. Desperation starts to seep out of your very existence, and rejection is rife. I knew I didn't want to go back to my former role in advertising, but what was I to do? I investigated doing a master's degree in positive psychology, but in the end, I had to ask myself what I really wanted to do. How would doing this change my life? Where was I going with this decision? It was there that I landed on coaching, and I've never looked back.

When I started up my business, I realised that fresh out of graduating there wouldn't be a plethora of people wanting to book my services, which I think is often surprising to a lot of new coaches. The first year of my business was spent finding the confidence to speak up, and to publicly use my voice and face to market my services. I didn't actually use my face at all until about six months in, and it wasn't until I started working with a business coach that I started to use my voice too. I spent a large portion of my time questioning my credibility, comparing myself to others and wondering if I could actually coach anyone at all. Not a great recipe for a successful business. But this healing journey ended up being a large ingredient in the ultimate success of my business and my suite of coaching skills.

To develop self-worth, you have to love and believe in yourself first.

That sounds a lot simpler than it actually is, because sadly most of us don't love and accept ourselves for who we really are. Society pushes us into little boxes of what is acceptable and expected of us, and along the way we totally forget about what it is we actually might want to be.

My business was never going to take off if I didn't love and believe in myself. How could I expect other people to believe in me and my services if I didn't even believe in myself? I had to face up to that and do something about it.

Once I started to understand that I didn't love myself enough to think I had a right to be there, I began breaking down the emotional barriers I had spent years building up to protect myself. The years spent in advertising quietly managing my fears and doubts had essentially isolated me from building valuable working relationships and any confidence in my ability. I was too afraid to speak up for fear of judgment and believed that what I had to say wasn't of any value. Love is one of the fundamentals of human life. To love and be loved creates the connectedness that we need and crave to be fulfilled and happy. I had cut myself off from this because I had told myself I wasn't worthy of it.

Life is better when you know you are inherently worthy.

To create self-worth, we have to begin with self-awareness. I wasn't aware that I didn't love and value myself until I was left with no job and no desire to go back into the industry, I had spent the last twenty years in. When I looked at that more deeply, I had to ask myself why I had stayed in a job I essentially hated for so long. What it came down to in the end was that I didn't think I was talented, knowledgeable, or smart enough to do anything else. This realisation was a sad shock to me, but once I knew it, I could work on it.

To do this I had to start with identifying and aligning with my personal values. I had never stopped to ask myself this, but understanding what was important to me allowed me to step into a version of myself that felt authentic and genuine.

Getting clarity on why I was doing what I was doing, not just for the sake of helping others but also for myself, gave me purpose. I started to feel like I was worthy in the world and that what I had to share was of value to others. We all deserve to be on this planet, and we all have a unique set of skills that we can share with others. It was realising this that unlocked the mindset prison I had created for myself and allowed me to finally find my voice, not just in my business but for myself.

Showing up in your business means showing up for yourself.

You have to take action. I had to stop hiding behind my fears and face them. One of my greatest fears was public speaking. I would do anything to avoid it, but I knew that not having a voice in business was going to make it almost impossible for me to gain success, and I had to do something about it. So, I spent some time with a hypnotherapist to overcome that deep seated fear. I worked with a speaking coach, I joined toastmasters, and I wrote a keynote presentation and workshop on imposter syndrome, which I then went out and pitched to people.

When I first delivered my keynote, it was awful. I was incredibly nervous, and I felt like I rushed it. I read the whole thing from a word document, and I truly thought it was terrible. But I did it, have kept doing it and have faced and owned that fear.

Credibility was something else I really struggled with at first. To overcome this, I pitched myself and my keynote to anyone I could think of and presented it as much as I could. The more I did this, the more confident I became and the surer of myself. Your voice is one of your greatest tools. Developing mine allowed me to show authority in my niche and attract more clients. I now know that credibility comes from who I am and who I believe I am, not what someone else says about me. I had to actively stop comparing myself to others, and I had to instead remind myself that I deserve to be there.

Once I started believing in myself, I also stopped being apologetic about the pricing of my services. When you spend twenty years working for a company, it seems impossibly hard to find a price that you can say without being embarrassed at first. You have to ask yourself 'what am I really worth'. It's not easy when you have little self-worth to start with. By unpacking that, I realised my knowledge, perspective and experience in life is really priceless. Placing a value on your services becomes a lot easier when you reframe your thinking that way. Charging your worth means valuing yourself and valuing yourself comes down to how worthy you really think you are.

I suppose in essence, Dad was right – there is no room for average. We are exceptional. When you know that, your life and business will change to reflect it.

Move over plain Jane – we're climbing.

So, what can you do to develop more self-worth for you in your business, life, or career?

Here are my top five tips:

1. Take back your power

Give yourself permission to feel what you feel. Forgive yourself for not loving yourself and find something you do love about yourself every day.

Practice gratitude. Be your own number one fan. You may find this hard at first but when you affirm that you are loved, are enough and are worthy, over, and over, you will eventually start to believe it and in yourself. Focus on the good things in your life and say thanks for them daily, however small, and simple they are – like a good cup of tea, or clean air in your lungs – the more you build this practice into your daily life, the more you will notice that good and loving things are always happening around you.

2. Find your tribe

Surround yourself with people who inspire you, support you and pep you up when the chips are down. There is nothing like borrowed confidence from a group of loving and loyal people when you have none yourself. If you don't believe in you yet, find someone who does, and then use their belief in you to help build your own belief in yourself.

3. Connect to your values and your why

We often don't know what we want when we have no self-worth, mainly because we're too scared, we'll do it wrong, fail and be laughed at. So, start with listing down what you don't want, and then write the opposite of that – what you do want. Ask yourself: 'What do I really want?' Lean into it and be honest with yourself. It's your journey, and no one is judging you. Write it down, even if it sounds ridiculous to you right now. The only person you are duping is yourself. Get real with what you want, and then make it into a goal.

4. Stop being so hard on yourself

Your inner chat continues the negative self-loathing loop. Change the language you use to describe yourself and the situations you are in from 'I can't do it.' to 'I may not know everything I need to know right now, but I can find out'. Give yourself a break. We all make mistakes, and failure is an opportunity for learning. Focus on what went right and take time to reflect on your achievements.

Start a reassurance folder. Collect the evidence that shows what you are doing well, what you have been successful in and how you are appreciated by others. Save emails and text messages and write down snippets of conversations! Keep it all and refer to it when you find yourself reverting back to the judging, negative inner voice.

5. Challenge yourself daily

Believing in yourself takes courage, and this means facing your fears. This is especially important as a solopreneur. No one is going to do it for you, so you have to take the steps to make things happen. Whatever you are afraid of, someone else is afraid of it too. When it comes to sharing your face, voice, or product/service, just know that someone out there is waiting for you and your service to become available to help them. Connect back to why you started in the first place.

I know it's not easy to love yourself when you've spent years letting your inner voice talk you down and dominate your life, but if you don't start the journey now, nothing will ever change.

I hope that my tips go some way to helping you build confidence and belief in yourself and your business the same way they did for me.

May this be the first step on your climb.

RACHEL LOUNDS

Rachel Lounds is a confidence, life and mindset coach and imposter syndrome specialist, who helps women overcome self-doubt and imposter syndrome to reach their career and personal goals.

She is an associate of The Imposter Syndrome Institute, the world's number one source of imposter syndrome solutions, and is licensed to deliver the Rethinking Imposter Syndrome™ program. It is her mission to help professional women bridge the confidence gap and excel professionally and personally.

Rachel has over twenty-five years' experience working in advertising. She has always had a deep interest in human behaviour and positive psychology, and so, after quitting her job in advertising, she decided to retrain to become a coach and focus on the very real but detrimental consequences of imposter syndrome on female success.

Rachel trained with the Australian Institute of Professional Coaching gaining a Life Coaching Diploma in June 2020. She has a BA in English from Lancaster University, England, studied Introduction to Psychology at Monash University, and studied with the world leading expert in imposter syndrome, Dr Valerie Young, at the Imposter Syndrome Institute.

Rachel loves helping her clients power up their potential to ditch self-doubt, find their purpose, and maximise their careers and lives through one-to-one coaching, group coaching, and interactive workshops.

Connect with Rachel for a FREE consultation to talk about where you are, what you would like to change, and how to make that happen.

Connect with Rachel at www.poschologycoaching.com.

Embracing the Fear and Doing it Anyway!

Sally Green

For a lot of people, the hardest part about drafting a book is the getting started part. It's easy to produce excuses: I'm not creative enough, I don't have enough time, nobody wants to read what I write. The truth is, anyone can create a book if they set their mind to it. What separates published authors from those who dream of writing a book? They face their fears and do it anyway. They find courage and embrace it. Since I began this journey in 2020, I have been part of numerous anthology books, writing chapters – like this one. However, I have yet to author my own book.

For the past two years, I have been stepping outside my comfort zone and doing things that both scare and excite me. For example, podcast interviews, speaking at online summits, hopping on calls with people who are wildly successful, and most recently flying alone.

I have spent most of my life pushing my dreams aside because, who am I? I was the one with the excuses. I was the one who was a mess. I was the people pleaser, feeling the need to make the life of those around me easier, while overwhelming myself. I was the one saying yes when I wanted to say no.

Being able to embrace courage was realizing that it's okay to say no. That it's okay to invest in myself because I'm worth it. Throughout my life, there have been countless times when I've talked myself out of taking risks or accepting opportunities because I didn't think I could do it, or that I was not good enough. But what I've learned is that if you don't believe in yourself, no one else will. We often sell ourselves short by listening to that nagging voice in the back of our head that tells us we're not good enough or smart enough or whatever-enough. Guess what? That voice is wrong. You are good enough, smart enough, and everything-else-enough. I am still a work in progress and at fifty-nine, I am finally learning to put self-care first.

Being able to embrace courage is doing it afraid. There's an old saying that courage is doing something even when you're scared. One of my personal goals for 2023 is to write and publish my solo book. This means putting my story out there for the world to see. It can be scary to put our writing out there, because we don't know how it will be received. Will people like it? Will they hate it? There's no way to know for sure until we take that leap of faith and hit publish. But being courageous means embracing the fear and doing it anyway.

1. ***Believe in yourself***

This may seem like an obvious one, but you must believe in yourself before anyone else will. Your story is worth telling. You are the only one who can author your story, so don't let anyone else tell you that you can't do it.

In 2020, at the beginning of my self-improvement journey someone laughed at me when I told them I wanted to be a life coach. They said, "You have no degree or experience, who would hire you as a coach?" Normally this would have made me stop and say, they are right, and I would have stopped pursuing it. But something happened inside me that day and I walked away saying, just watch me!!! I have used that conversation as fuel ever since.

I am fortunate to have a husband and daughter who are amazing and support me. However, I have had to sit down with that voice in my head several times over the past couple of years and explain to it that

I am resilient, that I have value and that I can get through anything. There have been many times that I have wanted to give up, but then something would happen, or someone would connect with me and suddenly it was "You can do this! You've got this!!!" I have learned to trust myself and set goals. I have had to remember that by following my heart and believing in myself that anything is possible!

2. ***Set aside your fears and step outside your comfort zone***

It can be scary venturing out of your comfort zone. Whether it's trying a new food, going to a new place, or meeting new people, stepping out of your comfort zone can be daunting. Ahh…but comfort zones are meant to be a challenge! That's how we grow and learn new things about ourselves.

For many years, I was a comfort zone addict. I was content to stay in my little bubble, doing the same things day in and day out. Get up, feed the cat, go to work, cook dinner, watch tv, go to bed, rinse and repeat. In 2020 all that changed, I realized that if I didn't start pushing myself, I would never accomplish anything hugely significant in my life.

I realized that comfort doesn't lead to growth. To grow, we need to challenge ourselves and step outside that comfort zone. It can be scary, but that's where the magic happens. You become open to new experiences and new opportunities. You're forced to think differently and stretch yourself in ways you never thought possible. Once I started saying yes to things that scared me, my world opened in ways I never could have imagined. I met new people, tried new things, and learned so much about myself.

3. ***Baby steps, take your time***

I used to think that I had to make tremendous changes in my life in order to get results. So, I would try to go all-in on fad diets or crash exercise programs, only to find myself back at square one a few weeks later. Once I realized that changing small habits and making minor changes over a brief period of time was the key to lasting success, my life really started to change for the better.

In March of 2020, I looked in the mirror and realized that I was a mess. I had been really, really good at taking care of my business, and my family, but I was really, really bad at taking care of myself. So, I made the decision and started with something small that I could control, my diet. I looked up healthy recipes and started cooking them. I cut out sugar, bread, and alcohol. I noticed that I began to feel better.

Over the next few months, I implemented increased changes. I stopped watching television at night and started reading. I started getting up earlier in the morning and meditating. I invested money in me! I registered for online courses, I paid to be a speaker at an event, and I joined a mastermind. Due to those small habits, opportunities began to reveal themselves and I became connected to some amazing people.

4. Get help if you need it

Many people find themselves struggling at some point in their lives. whether it's with their personal relationships, their careers, or their health, everyone goes through tough times. When you're struggling, it can be difficult to see a way out. That's where a coach or mentor comes in. A coach is someone who can help you identify your goals and create a plan to achieve them. A mentor is someone who has already been successful in the area you're struggling in and can provide guidance and advice. Hiring a coach or mentor can be a terrific way to get the help you need to turn your life around.

For a long time, I prided myself on being strong. I was the one who helped others, never the one who needed help. Asking for help would admit weakness, and I was determined to prove that I was strong enough to manage whatever life threw my way. As I've gotten older,

I've realized that there's nothing wrong with needing a little help from time to time. In fact, it can be essential for reaching our full potential.

Now, I realize that if I want to take my life and my business to the next level, I need to invest in a coach or mentor. Someone who can offer guidance and support and help me identify areas where I need to improve. It's not easy for me to admit that I need help, but I know it's necessary if I want to achieve my goals. So even though it goes against my instinct, I'm committed to asking for help when I need it. It's the only way forward.

5. ***Let your light shine***

It takes courage to step into your brilliance. It can be scary to shine your light so brightly, and risk judgement from others. When you step into your brilliance, you become a beacon of hope for others. When you allow yourself to shine, you give permission for others to do the same. In a world that is often dark and discouraging, your light can make all the difference. So don't be afraid to let your light shine. Step into your brilliance and watch the world light up around you.

6. ***You are worthy***

Most people go through life without ever really stopping to think about their worth. They go through the motion day after day, never really questioning why they're doing what they're doing. But when you take the time to step back and reflect on your knowledge, your strength, and your abilities, it can be a notable change. Once you realize your worth, your life starts to change. You become more confident and content. You attract better things into your life. Your relationships improve, and you start living in alignment with your true self. When you know your worth, you no longer settle for less than you deserve. You start speaking up for yourself and setting boundaries. You stop tolerating toxic relationships and situations. You begin to live with purpose and intention.

It all starts with courage…

Courage to be yourself

Courage to risk fear of judgement

Courage to step outside your comfort zone

Courage to follow your heart

Courage to act

Courage to ask for help

Courage to let your light shine

Courage to change

Courage to follow your dreams

Courage gives you the strength to do things that may be difficult or scary, and it also allows you to be more authentic and truer to yourself. It can help you take risks that could lead to new opportunities and experiences, and it can also help you overcome challenges in your life. So, if you're looking for a way to make positive changes in your life, start by embracing courage. It could be the best decision you ever make.

SALLY GREEN

Sally Green is the Vice President of Author Development at Action Takers Publishing. She is a multiple times international bestselling author, a writing coach, and empowers women to go after their dreams and become self-care rockstars. She lives in Connecticut with her husband, Billy, and her three cats.

Action Takers Publishing's mission is to empower 5 million women and men to share their stories with the world to make a greater impact on the planet.

Sally is also an artist and enjoys teaching art classes at local retirement communities around Connecticut.

Connect with Sally at www.ActionTakersPublishing.com.

The Other Side of Courage

Shermain Melton

The year was 2001. It was 10pm on a Saturday night. I just got home from working a 10-hour shift. I opened the door to my bedroom and I'll never forget what I saw. It was like a scene from one of those movies where burglars have ransacked the place. Everything was in disarray. It was as if a hurricane roared through my room. The top mattress of my bed was turned to the side and halfway leaning on the floor. All of my dresser drawers were open to different degrees. It was obvious that they had been searched through extensively. I looked over to my VCR and my adult movie was gone. (In case you don't know what a VCR is, it is a piece of equipment popular in the '80s and '90s that could record playback movies. When the tape has played to completion, it is automatically rewound and ejected.) My mom found the tape.

My secret was no longer a secret. I'd been found out. My eyes started to water, my stomach began to ache, my heart felt like it was going to beat right out of my chest, I started to sweat, and the hair began to stand up on the back of my neck. My deepest fear came true. I was afraid that my life would be over.

My mind started to shift into overdrive. I was scared because there was a huge unknown in front of me.

Maybe you know what it's like to face the fear of uncertainty?

I didn't know what would happen next. All of my fears began to surface. Some of my thoughts were:

- Will they out me to everyone and force me to deal with the aftermath alone?
- Will they kick me out and make me fend for myself?
- Will they still love me or will it be some sort of fake love where they are nice to me in person and talk trash about me when I'm not there?
- Will people still truly love me once they know the real me or will they walk away in disgust?
- Will people at my job find out? How will this affect my career? Will I be treated differently now or even fired?
- Do I have the courage to actually stand up, be myself, and not hide this part of me any longer?

In front of me was an opportunity to have a courageous conversation with my parents. I could have the conversation I'd been dreading to have for years, or I could run away from the situation. I could step up or step back. I had choices.

Maybe you know what it's like to run away from a fear for a long period of time because to stop and face it is acknowledgement that it does exist?

Fear doesn't like it when we shine light on it. It prefers darkness. Facing our fear requires courage.

Courage is derived from the Latin word cor, which means heart. We call forth courage to do things that feel scary to us. There are two definitions of courage that I like:

The first is doing the thing with all of your heart. The focus here is love. It is believing in your why or cause in your core, that it pulls you forward.

The second is doing the thing at the risk of your heart. It is knowing that rejection is a possible outcome of stepping into your fear and doing the thing anyway.

I grew up in a large Baptist household in Phoenix, Arizona. My dad was very involved in the church. There were ten of us: two parents, five boys, and three girls. I felt like just a number, unseen, and longing to be seen, understood, and loved.

I knew that my parents, friends, and family loved me, but I didn't know the depth of their love. I was unsure if it was conditional or not. I remember hearing stories from people in the gay community whose Christian parents kicked them out after they came out. They told them that they were on their own and disowned them. This was not love to me. There were conditions to the love that they received. I was scared to death of something like this happening to me. I just wanted to be able to live my life, be seen and loved for who I was. All of me. Unconditionally. I wasn't sure if I could trust my parents with my secret.

I decided that I would risk my heart and have the conversation with them.

The conversation with my parents ended with hugs and them saying, "We love you anyway."

I understand that the outcome of my story is probably in the minority for people who were of color, gay, and Christian the early 2000s.

Today, the main page of my website reads:

I am Shermain Melton.

I am Christian, Black, and Gay.

I hid most of myself for most of my life. If who I am doesn't resonate with you, that's OK. That's why I'm here. To help you be your authentic self, increase your visibility in the process, and grow your confidence.

I sometimes wonder if God made me as a joke. He gave me this big heart to love others so that I could experience the depth of not belonging. All I ever wanted was to belong.

I was told I couldn't sit next to someone at church because of the color of my skin.

Coming from poverty and feeling alone and lost, I chose to cultivate the courage to create a new destiny and identity for myself.

Now, I serve and teach what I wish I had for myself growing up. I will help you confidently and authentically live your truth.

I've created a community where you can belong, be yourself, be supported, be accountable, and cultivate your own courage so that you can create the positive impact you came here to give yourself and the world.

The story I told earlier was pivotal for my journey with courage.

As a professional leadership coach, I help my clients become more visible, more authentic, and more confident so that they can make the positive impact they have been longing to make.

I've created a tool to help you move from goal creation to action. Being in action requires courage. Break out a pen and write in this book (if you're moved to do so).

I will share a link in my bio to my website where you can download the fillable PDF version of this for yourself.

6 Ways to Build Your Courage, Become Greater, and Win

1. Make your goal real.

Get your goal out of your head and out into the universe. Communicate it to someone you love and trust. Something will shift inside you when you put it out there. The intention is not for the other person to hold you accountable. It is for you to practice being courageous with your voice.

Exercise: *Write down your goal. What is your goal? What impact will it have on: you, your family, your relationships, your organization, your team, your life?*

____

____

2. Shine light on your fears.

Acknowledge your thoughts and feelings. Your mind is good at creating outlandish stories to protect you. It can slow you down and even paralyze you with fear. Think about the scary goal you've created. Take notice of the thoughts and feelings that are coming up for you that are not serving you.

Shine the light on these fears, doubts, and insecurities. **Fear is afraid of the light. The light is inside of you.**

Exercise: *What are the top 3 fears, doubts, and insecurities that are the loudest for you as you think about your goal?*

____

____

3. Empower yourself.

Create a new empowering story. Think big here. Create your own empowering story that will excite you, make you smile, and cause you to want to step forward because of the importance and value of what you're stepping toward.

My goal is to grow my TikTok following to 100,000. Here's my empowering story example:

I woke up to a notification. The notification said that I was now at 100,000 followers on TikTok. I checked my email and received something from a follower. He thanked me for being courageous enough to talk about the things that mattered. He went on to say that because of my videos, he created a non-profit serving people of color in disadvantaged areas. His non-profit has helped 50,000 families. He invited me to come and tell my story.

I graciously accepted and spoke to a room of 2,000 people – helping them Be Greater. Saying yes to this opportunity allowed me to create a waiting list for clients. I never dreamed this would happen.

Your turn. Exercise: *Create an outlandish, exciting, and empowering story that speaks to what is created as a result of you reaching your goal, how you did it, what went right, and anything else that comes to mind. Get creative!*

---

4. Do the thing.

Take the small step forward. This won't be easy, but you can do the difficult things.

Exercise: *Write down what you're going to do. Make this a small step.*

---

5. Celebrate yourself.

Reach out to the person you shared your goal with and tell them that you did it! The goal is to celebrate your action, not the outcome of the action. Celebrate in other ways as well.

Most high performers skip this step. At a young age, we're told to encourage and celebrate others, to not boast or shine light on ourselves. It's OK to celebrate yourself. Do it now; do it often. Please don't skip this.

Exercise: *If you're choosing to celebrate yourself in other ways, list them here. How will you celebrate yourself?*

---

6. **Recharge your batteries.**

Take care of yourself. How are you feeling? Don't forget that what you did required courage. If you need to recharge your batteries, do that. Take care of yourself. Nobody is going to do it for you.

Exercise: *Write down how you will recharge your batteries.*

Example of how to use the 6 Ways to Build Your Courage, Become Greater, and Win.

Make your goal real

Example: My goal: To create a community of 50,000 people committed to going all in and being better today than they were yesterday. In this community, people will feel like they truly belong, can be themselves fully, can be challenged, can do things that feel scary, and come back and celebrate the tiny action they took.

I will feel supported, hopeful, proud, and joyful, and anyone I come into contact with will also feel this. The 50,000 people will impact others and, thus, my impact becomes exponential. I'll be able to give back to my community financially, travel more, and create more space in my life.

Shine light on your fears

1. Who am I to create this community? Nobody will join.
2. What if I don't reach that goal? What does that say about me?
3. Can I even do this?

Empower yourself

Already has an example.

Do the thing

Before Tuesday, I will send an email and post on social media inviting people to my new community.

Celebrate yourself

I will celebrate my small action by walking alone with no phone or other distractions.

Recharge your batteries

To recharge my batteries, I will wake up early and sit outside with my cup of coffee.

I chose to stop collecting evidence that supported my fear of not being enough. We do that sometimes, don't we? We collect evidence that supports our fear instead of collecting evidence that supports our ability to get things done, i.e. taking action.

I leave you with this:

Everything you want is waiting for you on the other side of courage. Go get it. Nobody is going to do it for you.

SHERMAIN MELTON

Shermain Melton (He/Him) is the founder and Chief Courage Officer of Courage to Impact. His mission is to help people be more courageous. He is an Executive Leadership Coach and he supports leaders who want to be more authentic, more visible, and more confident so they can make a more significant positive impact.

Shermain's clients are experts at serving others and he helps them cultivate the courage to prioritize themselves, slow down, and become the leader they've always admired. He is based in Phoenix, Arizona, and most of his clients don't need a coach but realize that to get to the next level they require new thinking and resources.

Shermain runs transformational programs to help leaders create more joy, freedom, and results. He is a Black, Christian gay man who is debt-free and chooses to be courageous every day. An IT nerd and business expert by training, Shermain has a background in Information Systems and Business Leadership.

For more than 25 years, Shermain has been a leader, coach, consultant, teacher, and trusted advisor. He earned his bachelor's degree in Computer Information Systems and an MBA specializing in small business and entrepreneurship. Shermain hosts a Courage to Impact podcast, which has a mission of provoking and inspiring people to be more courageous in their own lives. He is a Certified Professional Coach through the Institute of Professional Excellence in Coaching (IPEC), a certified MTBI Practitioner through The Myers-Briggs Company, and a Certified Professional Leader through PeopleTek Coaching.

Download Shermain's fillable PDF mentioned above called 6 Ways to Build Your Courage, Become Greater, and Win by visiting the resources page on his website at https://www.shermainmelton.com/.

Badassery!

Sue Gayle

This is the terrifying story of how, while attempting to adopt my two children, I came close to going to jail.

Have you ever heard the phrase, "don't ask, don't tell"? This became U.S. Military policy under the Clinton Administration in 1993. The policy prohibited military personnel from discriminating against or harassing gay applicants. I was not in the military, but as an American and a lesbian born in the early '60s, I lived my life hiding my sexual orientation from everyone, hoping that no one would "ask" me if I was gay and fearful that one day I would have to "tell."

Having to "tell" became even more frightening in 2004 when I went into Russia to finalize my children's adoption, even though it was illegal for me to do this as a gay woman.

I made the decision to adopt after having had a full hysterectomy. It was exciting to start looking into adoption agencies. My partner and I quickly found out gay civilians were not in the "don't ask, don't tell" category; gay people were classified in the "hell no" category. The adoption agencies even had it listed that gay persons were not eligible for adoption on their brochure. This of course was much different than it is today. Back then, most victories I had as a gay person happened quietly without raising red flags. I didn't have time to focus on the injustice of prohibiting a gay person from adopting a child; I was 42 years old and if I didn't adopt now, I would never be able to. Running out of time was my motivator and led to taking serious risks.

On St. Patrick's Day, March 17, 2004, we mailed all the required documentation to start the process. I only had a choice between Russia and Guatemala. Neither were at all gay friendly. Eventually, I chose Russia as I felt slightly safer there than in Guatemala. After that day, I was on my own. Since Russia was not gay friendly, my partner could not participate in the adoption. I had to take months of parenting classes, filling out reports, and all the interviews were me...alone.

In time, we got a call that a caseworker had to come to our home to verify it was suitable for a child. We scrambled to make my life partner into my business partner and (wink, wink) housemate. We set up a separate wing of the house to look like her area. We then went room by room and got rid of anything that showed us looking like a couple. We even completed a property quitclaim deed, removing her legally from our home. Publicly, in business and even in my family, it was normal for me to hide or not flaunt my relationships. This was mostly to make others feel more comfortable and for me to fit in. Now, here I was in my own home, my personal safe space, having to hide who I am and having to push down those feelings of indignity that were inside of me.

When the caseworker came, we thought we were really good actors, but after a while she asked, "Do you have something you need to tell me?" We played dumb to where she was going and then she proceeded to tell us about her gay brother. We continued to play dumb thinking it was a trick to expose us as the frauds we were. Luckily, in the end, she never exactly came right out and "asked" and we never fully had to "tell."

We finally started to get referrals from Russia. They would mail us a small packet on each of the children. The first eight children I declined because they all had numerous siblings and I did not want to separate the siblings. We heard that the Russian Ministry in charge of adoptions was frustrated that I had not taken any of the referrals and that I was behaving like a bad mother because these kids needed homes. As much as I wanted children and as much as I felt the pressure of the clock ticking faster and faster, I didn't want to separate siblings, so if that meant no children, then I would have no children. It was more important for me to not separate siblings than the "bad mother" shaming I was receiving from the Russian Ministry.

We had a six-week gap after that with no referrals and no communications. With every passing day I wondered if my dream of becoming a mother had ended abruptly. Then, in the middle of October, a packet came in the mail. I was by myself in my office when I opened it. As soon as I looked at their pictures, I knew…these were my kids! I got goosebumps. I couldn't catch my breath. When I went to show my partner the packet, my legs were shaking, making it hard to walk. In the packet were a soon-to-be four-year-old girl and an almost six-year-old boy. They were biological siblings with no other family members still living. They were true orphans. A pair.

Wow, the day had finally come. I was going to be a mother of not only one, but two, children! I must have read that paperwork 20 separate times and saw something different each time. Both children had multiple medical issues. A Russian family had adopted them but had returned them as "wild" children. Six months earlier, the children's mother had been killed by her boyfriend. Their father and other blood relatives had been gone for several years. None of that phased me. I just knew that I needed to get them and bring them home.

It was time to sign the official paperwork. I was super excited and reading those documents as I was eager to submit them back and confirm that these orphans would become my children. Then there it was…the place on the document where I had to declare I was not gay. Ugh! Geez, I had gotten so far without any direct confrontation. I've seen the kids and I know we are supposed to be together and *now* they ask me the question. I was a little stunned as to what I should do. Russia has a follow-up program after every adoption. They require every six months for three years a caseworker to come to your home and investigate, then report back to them. Will I go to jail if they find out? Can they take the kids from me later on if they find out? This required a little rocking in my chair and a lot of deep breaths as I stared at the paper deciding to sign or not to sign. As I pressed my signature to the paper, I thought about how easy it is for some women to have a child and how complicated my journey has been both physically and by social norms. Regardless of these challenges, I was ready to fight in my own way, for my right to be a mother.

My flight to Russia was set for November 19. I have four siblings, all of whom are straight, except my younger brother, who is also gay. I am so thankful he stepped up and agreed to go with me. Once we got over there, I wasn't sure if he was going to make it through the entire trip. If being gay flying into Russia was not scary enough on its own, between the two of us, we had $40,000 in crisp $100 dollar bills strapped to our stomachs to pay for certain steps of the adoption. Starting with the way we got through customs. I prepaid for a Russian escort to take us through an expedited customs process. We were selected out of line and walked in silence down this super long hallway to a small, dark room. The escort did all the talking to the guards, while my brother and I were nearly passing out from fear of knowing about all that cash on us. After an eternity, we entered Russia.

We initially stayed at the Marriott Grand in Moscow. My brother and I were so hypersensitive about what was happening that we even thought that they may have our rooms bugged.

We flew another three hours further in-country and were able to meet the kids for several hours with an interpreter. My soon-to-be son walked in the room with his little hands in his pants pockets. He was shy, sat down and started reading a book. They told me he is very calm, obedient, and loves to learn. Soon my daughter-to-be came in. They said she is not so shy. She came in and started talking to everyone freely. I learned she loves to dance, sing, and will do this at any time. She will be a challenge to settle down and has a TON of energy, with a will of her own. I needed to be ready. I had been concerned. What if they didn't like me, or worse, rejected me? What if they don't like the toys I brought? As soon as they walked in, that feeling was gone and was replaced with an overwhelming sense of calm and love. I had an internal knowing that we were destined to be a family. I didn't even wait for the doctor who was going to perform physicals on them the next day. I signed the official paperwork to request permission to adopt my kids with the Russian Ministry…Just like that, I'm PREGNANT!

Three days later, we found we had to leave Russia and come back in a few weeks to pick up the kids. I didn't understand and requested to stay. They firmly stated, "no, you must go." I don't know where this came from, but I firmly replied, "We are staying. I am on a 90-day business Visa and I want to spend time bonding with the kids." After a phone call, our escort came and told us to pack our bags and that we were leaving. We did not know where they were taking us. Can you imagine how frightened we were? Thankfully, they ended up driving in the direction where the kids were.

On the drive, we came upon an armed check point. There the chaperones instructed us not to speak a word. We waited anxiously in the car. We could see the driver and passenger escorts were in a panic state. The driver got out of the car and walked over and spoke to the guards. The female passenger was still in the car, looking at her feet, mumbling softly to herself. She was praying. The fear in everyone was so visible and time felt like it slowed down. My body was almost frozen in place. I couldn't stop looking at the driver and I could barely breathe. Finally, after the driver paid cash to the guards, they allowed us to continue on. In the car, the silence as we drove forward was incredible. We all knew if the armed guards found out we were Americans, or they found that large amount of money, they could have put us in jail or killed us for any reason.

After spending a couple of weeks seeing the kids every day at the orphanage, it was time to go to court and make it official. Instructed on how I had to present myself to the judge, I knew not to ever take my eyes off the judge as this was a sign of disrespect. I must always look forward even while the translator who would be standing next to me was talking in my ear. If I were disrespectful or untruthful, I could go to jail right there inside the courtroom.

My hearing lasted two and a half hours. The judge spent a lot of time on me being a single woman and had me explain how I was going to manage raising the children physically, emotionally, and financially. The Orphanage Director and the kids' Social Worker gave great testimonials of me and my interactions with the kids. Toward the end, the judge wanted to know if there was anything that I needed to disclose before she made her decision. This was the only time I could feel my face flush, become unnerved inside, and that I wanted to look away from her, but I couldn't. I said, "no," but inside I felt like she knew I was gay, but she didn't directly "ask," and I didn't "tell."

Court adjourned. We waited for about an hour or so to get the verdict. When they called us back to court, the Judge went through a list of statements and then she said, "I am granting your petition to adopt, and she inserted my kids' new legal names. Let me wish you all the success in the world and it is my honor to be the first to call you Mama." Talk about a hard swallow! She came off the bench and hugged me so hard! We both had tears in our eyes. What a moment!

Little did I know, this experience would define so many courageous acts from so many people, in so many different ways. Each of these demonstrated, whether it was big or small, how we can overcome an obstacle for something greater to happen. You may never know the full impact you have on someone's life, just as these people don't know what they did for me, but every day in every way we can take small steps that eventually move mountains, especially when it helps someone else in need.

My children are grown up, thriving adults and I AM one proud Mama.

SUE GAYLE

Sue Gayle is an entrepreneur, a founder and CEO of multiple businesses, a mother of two children and a genuine animal lover. Sue lives in Florida where her businesses are based. She has enjoyed the lessons of the relationships established with multiple Fortune 500 companies, her children, her dogs, and the other amazing people who have shared their lives with her.

Having the Courage to be MAGICAL

Suzanna Magic

As a child I was very sensitive and distant. I often felt as though I did not really belong here on planet earth. I had many weird experiences which I now understand to be spiritual experiences. I experienced being out of my body, astral travelling, seeing spirit, déjà vu, past life flashbacks and vivid dreams. I was called Dolly Daydream, considered stupid, and made to feel as though I was not making enough effort to be like others!

I was quiet but listening and the 'inside me' knew I was wise!! At high school I showed some promise but was never really credited with being clever—even when I achieved very high grades.

In my search for greater understanding of human kind I studied science, graduating with a BSc. honours degree in Biochemistry.

I felt called to teach after an interesting experience! As I was walking around the university campus one morning wondering what I should do next in life, I felt as though I had walked into a golden space teleporting me to another dimension and I heard the word 'teach.'

I followed this guidance and enrolled to do a teaching certificate.

I taught science in high school for several years often wondering 'what do the children really need to know?'

I've never really followed the 'norm' always doing things my way and have been called weird, strange and mad!

My life has been one of courage – surviving ridicule, put downs, challenges whilst leading the way or taking light into dark and difficult place.

Alongside my teaching I developed an interest in complementary therapies.

I had a major 'breakthrough' which led me on a search for greater understanding and eventually into healing training. This nurtured my gifts of intuition and insight and I learnt how to work with energy. I qualified as a healer and continued to develop my gifts and spiritual understanding, studying Colour Therapy and Crystal Therapy. I sat in a development circle for many years before starting my own groups. I now own my magical gifts, my empathy, my inner wisdom and use them to nurture other empaths to understanding, recognising, accepting and honing their spiritual gifts.

My teaching became focused on children with 'special needs,' many of whom disclosed their spiritual gifts. I have worked with a broad spectrum of ages, needs and abilities. All those I have worked with responded positively to being accepted, heard and nurtured.

In my current practise, I draw upon all my experiences and skills as mother, teacher, healer, intuitive and therapist. My soul purpose is to foster an understanding of spirituality and soul journey, help release old patterns, and nurture individuals on their journey towards fulfilment of their soul purpose. My current work is focussed on channelling DIVINE FEMININE ENERGY and Goddess wisdom, which is returning to earth at this time, helping others embody these energies.

I set energetic grids to reactivate sacred sites around the world when called to do so.

Here are some of the moments I found my courage to be magically me described in poem and story form!!

Courageous Healing Experience

While I was training to become a colour therapist I befriended a young man who lived near me. We would meet to swap treatments, practice what we had been taught and compare our experiences.

One day I phoned this young man to arrange meeting up for a swap and his flatmate answered the phone. Alas my young friend was not at home so I explain who I was and left a message asking him to please phone me back.

My friend did phone back and to my surprise he told me his flatmate had said that on hearing my voice he knew he had to come and see me for healing. I subsequently arranged a healing session with the flatmate as my client.

During the healing I could see I was clearing layer upon layer of dark energy from around my client. Suddenly there appeared the image of a black prince dressed in full length dark black armour and wearing a dark helmet. I realised this Dark Prince entity was encasing my client's body, something I had not encountered before. I had to find the courage to continue with the healing by letting my soul rise to the occasion and automatically do what had to be done.

Intense bright light focused through my hands and third eye upon the Dark Prince entity until it cracked away leaving my client free. I continued to focus bright light to guide this dark entity to the light.

A few days later my client phoned to thank me for the healing session. He said he had known he was 'possessed' and felt as though he was being chased for 3 years but had not known what to do about it. When he heard my voice he 'knew' I was the person to help him.

After the removal of the dark entity doctors had been able to diagnose organ stress and help this young man to recover.

The experience of encountering a Dark Prince was rather scary and challenging but my soul took over and I found the courage to continue and remove the entity.

Being in the right place at the right time to help a grieving mother.

One day I went to visit a very good friend of mine. When I arrived at her home she was engaged in a deep, quiet conversation with another lady friend of hers who I had not previously met. I said a brief 'hello' then tactfully withdrew to another room so as not to disturb their obviously private and personal conversation.

After chatting for about half an hour the lady stood up, introduced herself to me, thanked me for waiting quietly, said goodbye and left.

My friend thanked me for my tact and patience and explained that her friend had recently given birth to a baby boy who had sadly only lived for three days. This mother was very distressed and in had been in need of solace and support.

About an hour later the bereaved lady returned to the house and asked if she could talk to me. I was very surprised and wondered why she wished to talk to me. We sat and chatted. I listened whilst she shared with me her story. She told me about her baby boy's sad passing and asked me if I would be willing to go with her now to see the baby's body in a local Chapel of Rest. I was rather taken aback by this request wondering why she had asked me to accompany her. I summoned up my courage, rose to the occasion and, of course, agreed to go with her.

As we walked to the chapel she retold and expanded her story about her baby's birth, three days of struggling to live and his recent passing. She explained she was looking for answers and understanding before deciding where to bury her little boy. She and her husband were both from different countries, neither of them were from the UK where they lived now. Her husband's wish was for his son to be buried beside his deceased relatives in a family grave in his home town. Their other option was to bury the baby here in the UK near them as his immediate family but they worried he would be alone with no extended family to care for his soul. She felt she needed some guidance and clarity before making such a difficult decision and wished to revisit the baby in the chapel of rest.

On arriving at the Chapel of Rest, I took a deep breath of courage, trusting I was being guided to do and say the right thing. She had asked me to accompany her as she had a feeling I could help bring clarity.

I entered the chapel with her to spend time together with her baby. After several minutes of silence she spoke and asked me, 'Where do you think his little soul is now?'

I had an instant vision of the baby sitting on the right hand of Jesus and dug deep to find the courage to share this vision with her.

'I had a vision your baby has returned to Jesus and is sitting on Jesus' right hand' I replied.

'Thank you' came her reply 'That's what my older son thought too. Now I know he is safely with Jesus I can move on and make a decision about where to bury him.'

She thanked me for taking the time to be with her and for sharing my vision.

We left the chapel of rest, hugged and parted.

A few weeks later I heard from my friend that the mother and father had decided to return to her husband's homeland and bury the baby in the family grave. I feel very privileged to have found the courage to play my part in supporting a grieving mother and blessed to have been given such a powerful and clear vision.

Poem about being magically ME..................

MAGICALLY ME !!

I am Mrs Magic
I am a mother, grandmother
friend, homemaker,
mentor, empath,
teacher, healer,
soul guide.

I have magical empathy,
Spiritual gifts, psychic powers.
I can tap into another's essence
Celebrate, welcome, nurture
Guide them.
On their soul journey
Here on Earth
And
In other realms.

I can soar through the universe
Visiting stars and planets
Gathering wisdom
Bringing understanding.

I channel light to others
and to the Earth
Promoting personal and
Planetary healing.
I have visions of times gone by,
Access to ancient wisdoms,
Karmic patterns
Akashic records.

I set light grids across the planet
Connecting sacred sites
Opening portals of healing
Creating a golden web
Around the world.

I work with Goddess energies
Moonlight
Crystals, colours
Helping the Divine Feminine
Return to Earth.

I LOVE and embrace being ME
I honour my gifts
And wish to share them
With many, many people
All over the world
And throughout
The Universe
To bring
LOVE
PEACE
HARMONY
FELLOWSHIP
COOPERATION
xx

SUZANNA MAGIC

Suzanna Magic is a teacher, healer, mystic, mother to three wonderful children, and grandmother to six precious grandchildren.

As a child, she was extremely sensitive and felt as though she did not really belong here. Suzanna had many 'weird' experiences which she now understands to be spiritual experiences.

Suzanna was quiet, but knew she was wise!! She graduated with a BSc. honours degree in Biochemistry and felt a calling to teach and has taught across all age ranges.

Suzanna followed an interest in complementary therapies qualifying as a Healer, Colour Therapist, Crystal Therapist, Counsellor, Play Therapist, and Child Advocate. She hosts psychic development circles, full moon meditations online where she channels Goddess energies and wisdom, crystal and colour energies to help bringing Divine Feminine energy to earth.

Suzanna is an Earth Healer. She is called to sacred sites to set energy grids which re-activate power points across the planet. She feels her soul-purpose is to foster an understanding of spirituality, nurture others on their soul journey, and bring Divine Feminine energy to earth.

Suzanna writes poetry about her spiritual experiences.

She holds a B.Sc. Hons. Cert. Ed., Member Healing Trust, Dip. Colour Therapy, Dip. Crystal Therapy, P.C. Counselling, Cert. Play Therapy, Child Advocacy.

Connect with Suzanna at www.suzannahealer.co.uk.

Following My Dream

Tamara D. Ulrich

My dream was to be a ballerina. After that I thought maybe I'd be a veterinarian. Other than those fleeting dreams of a little girl, I've always known I wanted to work with children. To be a mom! I don't even remember when I knew I was going to start a school. It feels like that was always the dream.

As I completed my degree in Child Development, I began working at a Montessori preschool. I even helped start a couple of programs. Having my daughter was a lesson in embracing courage, due to fertility issues. That's another story. After she was born, I provided care in my home to a few other children to help make ends meet. When she was about two, the dream to start a school bubbled up again, strong. Since I was doing home care, it made sense to expand and create a program in my home. First, I would need a bigger house. I began searching for something that would work. Nothing was coming together. The minister at the church I attended suggested that perhaps it wasn't supposed to be a home program. He suggested I petition the board to start a school with the church. I was so excited by the idea. It seemed right. This was it! I appealed to the board. They said no! How could this be? I was devastated.

A friend suggested if it wasn't to be there, which by the way was completely across town from me, there would be another place. That just seemed crazy! And way out of my comfort zone. It was daunting to consider stepping out into leasing a space and creating a more public program all on my own. There'd be so much bureaucracy to wade through. It would cost a great deal more. I didn't have any money! Something pushed me forward. On a whim I called Portland Public Schools and asked if they had any spaces to rent for a Montessori preschool program. It turned out there was a building they weren't using and were renting out to various businesses. It was less than a mile from my house!

At this point everything began falling together. I found out about SCORE, which offers free help to business owners. My mentor helped me create a business plan. I met with the city and began the mountains of paperwork. So many requirements. I even had to plant street trees even though it was an already existing business property, with trees. I met with the Early Learning Division, Sanitarian, and Fire Marshall. With a few hoops to jump, I would be able to get licensed. I needed to start ordering materials. Business plan in hand, I went to the bank for a loan. The loan officer laughed at me! She seriously laughed. Who did I think I was to borrow money when I had nothing? (Isn't that why people get loans?) So now what!?

Again, things fell into place. My mother-in-law offered me a small loan. My Uncle offered a line of credit via a credit card he wasn't using. I had a small amount available on my own credit card. I had startup funds! I was starting on a shoestring, but it was a start. Looking at what I needed to order, I couldn't believe how expensive everything was! My husband at the time, with the help of his brother, began building shelves and tables. I found a company out of Sri Lanka that made Montessori materials that were half the price of what I could get in the States. I placed my order for the basics. I can't even tell you the excitement of picking up that crate at the docks and opening my shipment of materials. Beautiful shiny new Montessori materials. It was becoming real!

Somehow, someway, everything continued falling into place. Child's View Montessori School opened with six children in September of 1988! I started to joke that I had a silent partner making sure everything came together. I don't consider myself religious, but I do have deep spiritual beliefs. It seemed like every time an obstacle came along, as I embraced the courage to keep going, the universe, God, a higher power, whatever you might want to call It, came through. This seemed to be the case throughout the life of the school. By the end of the first year, we had twenty children enrolled.

Going into our second year, I opened a second classroom. Then I got notice from the school district that they were taking the building back for public education in January. I had four months to find a new place. I began the search but was coming up empty. After everything, was this it? One year and done? Then one day my husband happened to drive past a church having a yard sale. Something possessed him to stop. He happened across the minister and told him my story. He suggested I attend the next board meeting, which was in just a few days, to propose leasing space in their large daylight basement. I went and checked out the space. It was even better than our current one. I attended the board meeting. I expected just the actual board, but the room was full. A lot more people than I expected! I felt like I was just stuttering and stammering; overtaken with stage fright and not doing well presenting my case. One of the members stood up and started talking about her daughter having attended a Montessori school. She talked about what a great fit it would be to their goals and missions, and that by leasing to us, bring in revenue to the church and provide a service to the community. The board agreed. Saved! It was as if an angel had been planted in the audience to help me out. (She became, and is, one of my dearest friends.) Now I just had to deal with the city, the Early Learning Division, the Sanitarian, and the Fire Marshall. Again. Each of these agencies had changes they wanted made and hoops to jump. And more street trees to plant. It was distressingly close, but we were able to move just in the nick of time.

Starting Child's View took courage! More than I knew I had. Being open to the possibilities and continuing even when the obstacles mounted. The need for this courage and perseverance continued throughout my twenty-four years as the head of school. On the very first parent night, my daughter came down sick. I had to go anyway. Two months into our first year, it became evident that this wonderful little school I had created, where my two-and-a-half-year-old daughter would attend and be with me, wasn't working for her. It was just too hard to share her Mama, and she became a monster child. I ended up having to take her to another program where a friend worked. (She loves to tell people how she was expelled from her own mom's preschool.) I would drive downtown, my friend would take her in with her because I was having to drop her off 15 minutes before their program started, then rush back to open my own school. This was not the plan! As we started the second classroom, my friend joined my program, and my daughter returned to be in her class. Again, things worked out. Over the years we endured the ups and downs of staffing, two recessions, a lice outbreak, the birth of my son, my return to school for a master's degree and additional Montessori certification, a remodel, my divorce, as well as the everyday obstacles any business goes through. It was a continual lesson in embracing courage! I learned that when I stayed open and in trust, things came together much more easily. When I fell into fear and let the stress take over, it became much more difficult. I'll be honest; I did the second more often than the first.

I was blessed with having a business where my children could be with me. Yet it was a challenge. They had to adjust to having mom near, but not necessarily getting to be with me whenever they wanted. They had to understand the same rules applied to them as the other children, even though the school was like their second home. I often had to work long hours while they played in a classroom. There were times I put them to bed at the school. It was all consuming. I joked that the school was my middle child. It was my baby, my dream. Yet there was a lot of blood, sweat and tears – literally -- with it acting out to get attention and competing with my other babies. Over the years I sometimes felt resentful for what I perceived the school took away from my kids. They're adults now. I once mentioned this and was so surprised to hear that they had only fond memories. They had never felt short changed. They were proud of me that I had gone after my dream. I had shown *them* how to embrace courage. All four of my kids (two came with my husband when I remarried) have worked in some capacity at Child's View, providing them with positive experiences. They've helped in the classrooms, with maintenance, and on projects. As a bonus, they are amazing with little ones. One summer my daughter was old enough to be my assistant. My son was too old for the elementary summer program, but not yet old enough to be 'real' staff, so he was our helper. Well, he'd say go-fer. It was the best summer having them work with me in the classroom. My daughter was one of the best assistants I ever had! I learned that my perceptions of the difficulties, and what I imagined were detriments, really weren't. As parents, one of the greatest gifts we can give our children is a growth mindset and the courage to be who they are. To follow their own dreams. What a joy to realize I had done just that by being true to myself, embracing courage, and following my dream.

After twenty-four years it was time to sell the school. I again had to embrace courage and trust the universe had my back. I had no idea how to proceed. As I opened the doors to the possibilities, the pieces came together. Again, SCORE came through for me. I put together a Business Sales Presentation Package and listed the school. I was soon contacted by someone interested. She was perfect! We connected. We were like minded. She'd continue the school with the same commitment to the Montessori philosophy with a strong connection to peace education and nature that was so important to me. But she had no money! It was so disappointing. How could she buy the school?

It turns out that she too was embracing courage, following her dream. Together we opened to the possibilities. We came up with a plan, put together all the legalities, and moved forward. We are coming up to the tenth year since I sold Child's View. It has grown from two preschool classrooms, to now including infant/toddler and elementary programs. Even through Covid. My dream continues! I had the courage to step out against the odds and difficulties, and the universe stepped out to meet me. That courage was again replicated with the sale of the school in an unconventional manner, and the new owner's courage to follow her dream.

I learned along the way that as I embrace courage, and step into trust, knowing the universe has my back, things fall into place. When I let the fear and stress run the show, life gets difficult. Oftentimes problems grow and seem insurmountable. My perception of the problems isn't necessarily what's real.

Not only is this so important for us, but when we embrace courage, we provide a model. This is especially true regarding our children. We lift others up to embrace courage as well. We may think, who am I to do this? Who are you not to?

Since selling Child's View, my dream has changed a bit from working with children to working on their behalf. Making a difference for children and families continues to be my passion! I'm a Parent Coach, I teach Early Childhood classes at a local college, and I provide parent and teacher education and workshops. I love to create optimum environments for children, and to decipher the communication of children's behavior. Difficult behavior is communication of an unmet need. It's up to us to understand, then provide the nurture and guidance.

I'm now embracing courage once again by contributing my story to this, my first collaborative book. I'm also writing my first solo book. *The Guiding Mindset* supports parents in how, with a change in how we think about children, and the guiding principles, we can more easily work through the challenges we may face as parents. It's how we think about children as full little humans, how we guide them to become who they are truly meant to be, and to experience the joy children bring to our lives, hearts, and homes. I'm again stepping out in trust, knowing the universe has my back.

TAMARA D. ULRICH

Tamara Ulrich, MA, is the founder of Educating the Essence and is a Parenting Coach, Educator and Consultant. She is passionate about making a difference for children and families; empowering parents and teachers to experience the joy children bring more fully to our lives, hearts, homes, and classrooms. Her mission is to support and empower parents and educators to nurture the essence within each child into the blossoming of their full potential and being.

Tammy also teaches Child & Family Studies courses at a local college and provides workshops and trainings for parents and teachers. With over thirty-five years of experience working with children, families and educators, Tammy has worked in a variety of capacities, including Founder and Head of School of Child's View Montessori School. She holds OPEC Parenting Educator Recognition. She serves on the Oregon Montessori Association Board as Secretary and is a past President and Executive Director.

Tammy lives with her husband and two adorable labradoodles in Oregon. Her four amazingly awesome kids are now grown, and she loves being 'Gammy' to two incredible little humans.

Connect with Tammy at https://edessence.com.

Embracing Courage

Tamara Fraser

What comes to mind when I say the word "courage"? There are many words and people that come to the forefront of my mind when I hear that word. I can tell you with 100% certainty, though, that when I think of the word "courage," I do not think of me. I haven't dug deep enough to unearth the why behind this yet; I just know it is not how I think of myself. I know in my heart that I have had many moments in my life where I've had to embrace courage; I am just not 100% convinced that even with these courageous moments I would describe myself as courageous.

Perhaps one of the reasons I don't see myself as courageous is because for all my life I have struggled with self-worth. (**What I'm about to share might cause a trigger within you.**) At the very young age of 2.5, I was sexually assaulted by a babysitter. This happened again when I was nine with a different babysitter, but I believe the trauma of the first experience is what has prevented me from truly believing that I am worthy. When words like "you will be hated for what you did" and "I will kill your family if they find out" were imprinted in my brain at such a young age, it turned my everyday life from one of thriving to one of surviving and in that survival mode, there was a constant need to cross my "t"s and dot my "i"s in order to accept the love that I had in my life.

When I try to see myself as a model of courage for those around me, the voice in my head starts telling me that I am being boastful and arrogant. It cautions me from seeing myself this way so that I don't become too big and too much. It's almost like I have this little program written into my hardware that ensures I stay below a certain threshold and, therefore, I avoid reaching for my true potential.

Pushing past this limiting threshold every single day of my life is how I would say I have embraced courage in my life.

I was sitting with my social worker in a session one day relatively soon after she had encouraged me to start running and she asked me, "Tamara, do you see how much power your abusers have in your life?" I had never thought about it this way and it was so overwhelming to start recognizing where they were showing up in my life and how frequently they were there. There are times when I think back to these "aha moments" where I am so incredibly angry. How can one human being (or in my case two) steal a child's life and weave so much trauma into their being that at the age of 47 they are still trying to unweave the trauma? Choosing to be a cycle breaker is one of the areas in my life I know I have embraced courage. I will not be a victim and have that dictate my life. We made a plan that day in my social worker's office. From that day on, I was going to start taking my power back and, in the moment of that decision, I started my journey to find and one day love me.

The first step to reclaiming some of my power was to embrace the anger that would consume my body when I would have these "aha moments." My social worker encouraged me to write their names on the bottom of my feet before I went for a run so that with each step I took, I was literally stomping them out of my life. I did this for several years and every race I ran, you can be sure that I had one name written on the bottom of each foot. When I would feel myself fading in my run and the self-talk of quitting started kicking in, I would think of the names on my feet and say to myself, "not today you don't – today I win."

In those early stages of accepting my story and learning to unravel the fabric of the trauma from my definition of me, every day felt like a courageous act. There were so many moments I didn't want to continue. So many moments I wanted to just disappear. I would be driving to counselling and plucking my eyebrows out one at a time so that I could distract myself from driving off the road and feel something different than what I was feeling. Maybe if I could just "disappear" life would be easier for me and everyone around me? Maybe I wasn't ever going to see a light at the end of the tunnel and this mountain of hell was never going to go away? I knew in the depths of my soul that I wouldn't follow through with wanting to disappear. At the same time, though, there were so many moments that I remember thinking, "I can't do this. I am not strong enough to do this."

Looking back on those years, I can clearly see how I embraced courage every day. I forced myself to run even when I didn't want to. I forced myself to go to counselling even when I hated it. I forced myself to take my medication even when it made me feel numb. I forced myself to go to work even when I could barely make it through an hour without crying. I forced myself to take care of things around the house like laundry and groceries even when all I wanted to do was sleep. Most importantly, though, I forced myself to open my heart and love my babies fiercely even when I doubted my ability to care for them and their ability to love the real me. Every day something that I experienced with them kept me going even when everything inside wanted to just give up. Every one of these simple tasks was me embracing courage. Yet, in the moment, they all just felt like "to-do's" in a never-ending list of the obligations of being alive.

Have you ever sat on one of those plastic woven fabric lawn chairs and noticed the various colours of the fabric? What if you despised one of those colours? What if every single colour in that fabric was one of your favourite colours except one? Would you try to unweave that colour from the chair? That's what this phase of my life felt like. I was literally unweaving one colour from the fabric of my life. Maybe it was gray …. maybe it was brown …. whatever the colour it was, it didn't go with who I am and so every single day I embraced the courage to unweave that colour from my chair, from me.

I remember in counselling one day my social worker had me write down a list of words describing how I viewed myself from that time as far back as I could remember. I filled a notebook with words and I think over 97% of them were extremely unkind words. I didn't have many nice things to say about myself. She then typed up all of these words for me and we created healing projects out of them.

One of the projects was to create a memory box. The inside and outside of the box were covered with photos of me over my life. On the outside of the box, I asked a few of my close friends to also make a list of how they saw me, and I was to write those words on the outside. My words went on the inside. I still have this box in my closet, and it is a constant reminder to not always believe the voices in my head because the voices often read the inside words.

Another project was for me to take these "outside" words and have some friends paint them on my body. For someone whose love language is physical touch, this was an incredibly powerful experience for me. I got to see and feel these words on my body.

The final experience for me was to create "dolls" with my "inside" words shoved inside of them. We then had a funeral for these two dolls so that I could separate "them" from me even further.

This work was exhausting and often felt like it would never end. For most of these years, I felt like I was at the base of Mt. Courage and there was no end in sight. Over time I started resenting the counselling and the medication. I felt completely numb because the only anti-depressant that didn't make me feel like I was on speed made me feel numb. I was also so tired of constantly feeling like I had to fight. So, I quit both – just like that. I know now that I should have spoken to my doctor about stopping my medication. I also know that quitting something that was no longer serving me was incredibly courageous.

I believe there is a distorted perception of what courage and being brave mean. Being courageous is not the same as taking risks. Being courageous is making choices that serve us. Why would any human alive continue with something that wasn't serving them? By not truly listening to oneself, we make the mistake of turning off the gifts of intuition we were given when we were born. I didn't know at the time that what I was doing was courageous and I still wouldn't say "I AM courageous" – all I knew was that I could not go and re-live my trauma anymore. I also knew that the colour in the fabric of my lawn chair was fading, and I didn't like how that felt. I could not numb my feelings anymore. I needed to feel alive; to feel vibrant; to *feel* again, and so I quit.

Looking back on my life, I see many acts of courage every day. Some were tiny steps, and some were massive. For me, the most massive step I have taken though is walking away from love. I still don't feel ready to share this experience and maybe I never will. What I will share is that walking away from someone I loved so very much took a long time and was one of the most difficult decisions I have ever made. I know that I made the best decision for my life because even though I loved so very much, it didn't feel like love in return. I appreciate that all relationships are work – for me, though, love shouldn't feel hard. I have this picture in my mind that love should always feel like coming home and I'm not sure I've ever felt that way. So, I chose me. I chose my kids. And I chose to work on liking me more so that perhaps one day I will eventually love me enough to feel like I'm home.

After thinking back to some of the times I have embraced courage, I have realized that courage for me is not taking risks that feel wrong in my body, nor is it having blind hope that if you love big enough everything will be ok. Courage for me is the small steps we take each day to listen to our intuition, to learn to love ourselves, and to shine our authentic light. Courage for me will always mean peeling off the layers until I can get to the core of who I am and truly reach my full potential. And finally, courage for me will be ending each day being able to look myself in the eyes and smile at myself knowing that I did my best and lived in a way that makes me proud.

Mt. Courage is not meant to be climbed in a day – it is the mountain we are destined to climb for life. I promise to continue to climb even if there are days I can only take one step. Perhaps, just by doing so, I will start to see myself as courageous and truly worthy of all that I dream of.

TAMARA FRASER

Tamara Fraser is a busy single Mama of three beautiful teenagers. She is a teacher, Zumba Instructor, and Health & Fitness coach. She loves helping busy Mamas make themselves a priority in their own lives and is on a mission to change the narrative on Moms putting everyone else first. She believes that all of us need to fill our own cups first so that we have more light and love to share with others.

Connect with Tamara at https://www.instagram.com/freetobetam.

Living with Grit and Grace

Teaira Turner

The room rose on its feet, the crowd grew silent, I jerked my head from side to side, flinging the sweat from my brow, like slow-motion, I faintly hear the referee. "YAMEEEEE." Get outta my way ref. Ima get him before he gets me. Think smarter. Faster. Faster than the fastest competitor. I only see red. I'm remembering the wet smell of rust. My mouth, my head, all wet. Salivating, as if I'd never eaten before, relentless hunger for annihilation. This poor kid. Had no idea. He goin' learn taday!!! I can taste the fear in his bright eyes. It tastes good. "Do y'all eat rocks for breakfast?," a distant voice asks. I feel a sick sense of pride emitting from my corner, yet they hope he makes a full recovery (sort of). Slowly backing away, still with the neck of his Gi in my grip, I slowly remove myself from between my opponent and the ceiling. My mouth is still wet. Eyes locked in. Zanshin. Rust smelling liquid dripping from my mouth. I AM LUNAAA!!!!

In my "I don't do fashion, I am fashion motorcycle jacket with gold basket buttons and zippers creating an interesting juxtaposition suit," I stare at the words on the monitor. My manager's dress up, is my dress down. I'm constantly distracted from the monotone eggshell colored cheap paint on the walls. I see an urgent 15-minute meeting request sent for today @ 4:30 (it's 2:30 pm already) from my skip level manager (cc'ing my manager) "we would like to discuss your recommendations on the department's operational efficiencies along with your career trajectory at Drug Store Cotton Health System." I would not be defeated. Ten toes down. "Always," I say to myself. I click the Microsoft Word icon. All I hear is click, clackity, click, click, clackity click. Double tap. Click, clackity, click, click, clackity click. Eight minutes later, "Thank you for allowing me to grow as the Chief of Staff Administrator here at Drug Store Cotton Health System. Based on your proposed agenda topics, I have re-considered my professional and career trajectory. Please allow this to serve as my letter of resignation effective immediately." (My inner thought was 'I'ma get you before you get me!') That same red colored, rust smelling liquid pouring from my forehead is covering my fingers on the keyboard. My peripheral becomes a throbbing red glow again. Again, all I see is red. All I can taste is that blood. And again, I like it. My right pinky finger hovers over the closest key. In perfect form, I engage send… As I repeat to myself… I AM LUNAAA!!!!

Panicked, I jump up. Damn the 6:00 a.m. alarm. PANTING feverishly. Face, chest, everything covered in sweat. Another one of these dreams. Damn. Who am I chasing? Why am I always dreaming about "fighting"? Why are my actual past experiences reoccurring in my dreams? I thought dreams are generally altered. Nope. Not me! My actual experiences often show up in my dreams. Is someone after me? Why am I continuously letting these thoughts torture me? What exactly am I trying to win? Why can't I just chill? Who really am I fighting? Who is the competitor? Who am I in competition with? I jump out of bed, turn around and I pull the cold wet beater from my body. Ring the sweat from it. Pull the sheets from the bed. Toss in the laundry. Another cold sweat. Am I traumatized? Why do I have this insatiable desire to win? It's like an addiction. No matter what happens. No matter how awful or traumatic, I eat it up, never whine or complain. Never ever, ever will I play victim. Hell, only two people will know "the real" anyway. I eat this shit up, gobble it up, spit to out, eagerly looking for the next round. Who's next? What's next? How did I become desensitized to trauma? Yes, I wholeheartedly believe in myself. I know that my beliefs and capabilities directly influence my outcomes and trajectory of life, but?!?!?! At what costs? Is that always good? It's like I'm addicted to the chase. It's like I'm addicted to the conquest. But are those conquests traumatic? Do I really normalize traumatic experiences? What type of mindset welcomes challenges, looks forward to the next feat? The brain is a muscle. It grows. Has my brain grown a thirst for conquering the next feat? Is this some sort of addiction? Am I addicted to the next feat? The next challenge? Why? What killed that sympathetic part of my brain? Do I even have feelings anymore? Who normalizes trauma? It's like someone muted my mental 'CAUTION' notifications. The question is…WHO?

Somehow, it's already 7:15, I'm dressed and out the door. I drop the kids off to daycare and grab the last-minute items for my big GRADUATION!! "Teaira Turner - Top Graduate from the North Sciences School of Health Information Technology." I can hear it now. I'm getting butterflies in my stomach already. But chileeeeee. Whoooo baby!!! Wanna know how a person graduates TOP of her class, with a master's degree in Medical Informatics, without one lick of healthcare experience, after winning round after round in court after your newly deceased husband's mother attempts custody of your two-year-old twins, while managing three part-time jobs, volunteering work, AND MAKES time to care for herself? It is success or suicide? I wrote a short story about it. Wanna hear it? Here goes….

The answer is quite simple. I believe the new buzz word is "Growth Mindset." They said, "you can have anything you want in this world." They said, "If you can make it in New York City, you can make it anywhere," they said. "They can't break you because they didn't make you," they said. Well, while I am beyond proud to have come from where I come from in an era that's legendary, NO ONE ever laid out the long-term Trifecta plan on how to be successful, happy, and SANE. No one ever laid out the blueprint. They missed relaying that lesson.

It may have started when my 8th grade teacher, Mr. Crane, re-arranged the class and put me in the middle of the class because he thought I was the perfect emission of sunshine that the entire room needed?!?! Or perhaps, it started when my 10th grade teacher allowed me to teach my classmates geometry and trigonometry?!?! My classmates were my friends. Each one of them. I LOVED that they trusted me to help them understand my favorite subject. It was an intangible gift that I never took lightly. Maybe it was a slew of memorable undergraduate experiences. Was it due to a fast-track professional career in corporate America because the big wigs would say "I LIKE YOU!" MAYBE!!

(Sidenote: They need to start putting "likeability" on job requirements. It is a REAL thing.)

It's June 2012 and I am FEELING myself. Chileeeeee. You can NOT tell me I am not the cat's meow!! I can't wait to hear my name when I walk across the stage. Oh my. I am remembering the agony. The work. The sleepless nights. Reading and practicing my presentations to the nurses in the local Children's Hospital because one of my mini me's decided it was a great day for an ear infection. Straight A's…two consecutive years…twenty-one classes. and three part-time jobs later, I will have earned my master's degree in Medical Informatics. The reward for a tremendous effort. In hindsight, that's enough all by itself. If you add to the list being an involved, mentally present widowed mom of two-year-old twins while battling your deceased husband's mother for custody of YOUR kids!!! Baaaaaby!!! (But that's a longer story for another time.)

Rewind two years and welcome to my world where, daily, I clearly crave impossibility. They say repetition is the mother of all skills. I've said it so often that subconsciously I've grown to live this reoccurring theme, that yes, I can do anything! While I don't strive for perfection, I do aim for the stars. I might not get the stars, but I'ma get the moon.

I read the list of requirements: "To be eligible for Medical Informatics Graduate Programs, applicants must meet the following:"

"Cute." Who says cute? Like girl who do you think you are? "I am LUNA. Ten toes down. ALWAYS." I have the base requirements. That's undisputable. A four-year bachelor's degree from a regionally accredited institution in the United States or an equivalent international institution (blah, blah, blah). Okay, so that's three of ten requirements. CHECK. But this remaining seven of ten healthcare stuff, NOPE. Never worked a day in healthcare. NOPE, never managed three to five direct reports in a hospital setting. NOPE, not efficient in any electronic medical record system. NOPE. NOPE. And NO!

But! My good fella… What does she have? That's where I need them to focus! Here's the difference between me and the other candidates. I can show you how my transferable skills will make me more than just an excellent student in your program. Here is where things got real. How to manage my time effectively, establish a healthy work-life balance, while managing my stresses are huge challenges for graduate and professional students. My struggle was feeling like I'm not doing enough or accomplishing greatness.

And voila. Just two years later, I wasn't wrong! I knew I had a slight edge over most of my classmates regarding anything having to do with business and informational technology. Most importantly, I am business savvy. Having led these departments for ten years, I had experience. Not just any ole' regular experience, a Fortune 500 company recognized me as a high potential top performer early in my career. Shit, I was born exceptional. All I had to do was convince the right person(s) that this strength is valuable and needed. Also, I had to show the school that they needed someone like me with a slightly different background. What wonders they could do with a candidate with a diverse background. And once I did well, the school also looked good. Again, I wasn't wrong!

My deficiency was my actual healthcare experience. How do I get genuine experience? When do I have the time to get this experience in my new field? I volunteered. Who would turn away a professional adult volunteer. Surely, someone would oblige. After five interviews or so, I landed a volunteer spot in the PRE-MED program at the local VA hospital. I was in my glory. I also like to think, in general, I'll do what it takes to get the job done. Not sure how many people would interview five times for a volunteer role. So, what if I was ten to fifteen years older than everyone in my class. But my skin is melanated, so you couldn't tell. And just like that! Viola! Experience at one of the top healthcare facilities in the city. Again, so what if it wasn't a paid gig. That's called marketing. Don't blame me. I didn't create the game, but I understand the game ... and I came to play. And I play to win! Accepted in a "rotational" medical program, learning all about the different departments and health systems. This was great. After one year, I'm on a roll. I knew I was doing well when folks reached out to me quickly to be partners on class assignments. And sure, I'm used to school, but graduate challenges were completely different than those from my undergrad experience. Operating at high levels with competing priorities, mastering an effective and efficient work/school/kid schedule, social calendar for my sanity, identifying and burying potential threats before they become manifest into stresses. Sis!

After two years, it's time for graduation. What would have happened if I didn't have the growth mindset to see this from an optimistic point of view. What would have happened if I let the seven of ten requirements deter me. I learned that an optimistic, healthy mindset is critical. I heard a term that symbolizes how I operate that completely determines my accomplishments. A Growth mindset.

I learned and fully embrace that a growth mindset can directly influence a person's aptitude and accomplishments in life. I know the brain is a muscle and our intelligence and talents can grow. I believe the way we think about ourselves, and utilize our innate talents and strengths, has direct impact on our lives. I believe being honest with oneself particularly about the things we aren't so good at is critical to progress. So, if I had to bring life to my mindset, it would be through Luna. Luna, my spirit animal, the alpha wolf is significant because she represents who I am and how I move. One of her main responsibilities is bearing pups and raising the next generation. Since one of her main roles is to support her mate, the male leader of the pack, and hunting, Luna is arguably the most important female of the pack. "Luna" is Latin for "moon." Research has often connected the moon to femininity. Over time, the hunger for achievement, fueled by a growth mindset, can become an addiction. If not effectively managed, spiritual, mental, and emotional harm to oneself may result. It's become a matter of life of death.

I believe remaining available and acting on well-intended feedback directly influences our successes and accomplishments. I've learned that open and honest reflections often reveal information that guides our decisions. By no means am I attempting to create rules that govern how people should think, I'm merely expressing my mental disposition which is a result of my life's experiences. We are all entitled to be who we are. Optimistically, balance hope against naivety. Carefully, analyze the return on any investment. Strategically, execute your plan of attack (oooops, I meant action ☺).

I invite you to explore the differences between a growth mindset and a fixed mindset. I recommend several meditation sessions with yourself. Ask yourself, "How has my mentality influenced my behavior?" You may even consider inviting your trusted network into this exercise. I recommend taking personal inventory and really think about how you can positively impact your next decision.

So, after taking inventory and accurately assessing, utilize your trusted network for wisdom, and…

In perfect form…

LUNGE and REMEMBER LUNAAA!!!!

TEAIRA TURNER

As founder of The Ivy Eternal Enterprise (TIEE), Teaira Turner and team partners with artists to help them transform the 'business side' of their organizations for sustainability and prosperity. TIEE uses an end-to-end integrated approach in back-office operations, strategy planning and program execution. Empowering strategic partners to achieve their business goals and deliver optimal customer experience enables them to focus more by creating what they love. Strategic partners operate in Community, Health & Wellness, Education & Service (CHES) spaces.

Teaira is enthusiastic about incorporating a growth mindset in every aspect of life and advocating for health and education. Over the years, she has learned that the joy of others lies in ourselves. She works on other projects to help eliminate the disparity in education by providing the access and exposure to resources in the community. She has infused mentoring, educating, and networking into her personal and professional life.

Coupled with her twenty plus years in Business Management & Marketing, Teaira has an insatiable desire to help strategic partners achieve their highest potential. Teaira attributes her values and respect for the community to growing up in the Bronx in New York, graduating from a HBCU, excelling in corporate America, and working as a Healthcare Administrator.

While she resides in the northwest section of Philadelphia, Pennsylvania, Teaira is a native New Yorker and is avid about selfcare and maintaining a healthy lifestyle. She enjoys roller-skating, traveling, and exploring all things entrepreneurial with her teenage twins.

Connect with Teaira at

https://www.instagram.com/ivyeternalenterprise.

The Courage to Stand in My Truth as a Loving Daughter

Tina M Moreau-Jones

There are volumes written about how to help loved ones navigate through the end-of-life journey. There are more volumes written about working with family members through this most challenging time. Even more volumes still about self-care and well-being as a caregiver. None of these can be compared to the lived experience of immersing in the love and care of a dying parent.

If my experience of embracing courage can be a blessing to the reader, may it be so. This is a sliver of my journey as my family goes through the process of allowing my dad to die at home in the care of hospice.

After a great deal of prayer and trust in God's providence, my dad entered hospice care in the comfort and privacy of his home in the spring of 2022. It was a decision that he and my mom did not make lightly. At the time I write this, it is the end of summer in that same year. Hospice provides a weekly check in by a nurse and two weekly visits to bathe my dad. The family provides all other care.

As a natural born people pleaser and peace maker, and wanting to be all things to all people, I embarked on being present with a determination and a love in the confidence that I could do my part and we, as a family, could do it all ourselves. I mean, if my parents could pour their lives into raising me as a child, giving back in this way was the least I could do to allow dad to pass peacefully.

When running a 72-hour shift as a light sleeper, everything suffered– I lost myself in the process of losing sleep, being always on high alert to care for dad, and trying to help minimize mom's workload. My relationships suffered– no energy to talk or to connect. My career and income took a hit– no energy to reach out for sales. My marriage took a hit– Dan spent much of the summer alone. Even when I was with him, my mind was elsewhere…

As the summer wore on, my weekly four-day 24-hour shifts began to take a toll on me and things in my life began to slowly fall apart. I was viscerally watching my life begin to decline: my health (emotional, physical, mental, spiritual), my marriage, my career, my relationships. Without sleep and restorative rest, I was giving from a drying well and things began to suffer. I began to isolate and allow judgment to creep in. My soul was not at rest, even in doing my best to be a good servant to my parents and family. When my soul is not at peace, the rest of me is not at peace.

Eight months into hospice care, we are realizing this will be a lengthy process and continuing on with the way things were is unsustainable. I will have nothing left to give when my best will be most needed later on.

Here's where my story of courage begins. It takes courage to admit you need help. (No more, "I can do it myself, thank you" attitude!) It takes courage to step into the 62-year-old version of Tina who is not really known well by her family. They still know and see me as a younger version of myself, without the wisdom that comes from living a full life. It takes a boatload of courage to stand up for and reconnect to my most compassionate and powerful self and actually consider who I am, how God made me, what I am able and not able to do, be, and give, not for selfish reasons, but so that I will actually have more to give when I am needed most.

Standing up for myself means also owning the size of myself, in all my brilliance and imperfection. It means that not everyone will be happy with my decision but, if made in love and with deep care for others, God will honor it.

God has blessed me with many talents especially in the area of servant leadership. Making good decisions and leading others by example come naturally to me. This time, I am completely out of my comfort zone– there's no real playbook for accompanying your dad in the dying process and figuring out how to do it with each family member entering the experience with their own way of being and ideas of what's the best way to move forward. I was a mess, and I reached my limit so… I took a bold leap of faith and… I reached out for help. I REACHED OUT FOR HELP! And in help has come relief and release.

Help came in the person of my husband, Dan. Dan and I took out our calendars and looked at the fall season. With much prayer, deep love, and seeking God's Will in the decision, we jointly marked out the times I could be available to take shifts, making sure to carve out time for us to be together and nurture our marriage. This new schedule allowed for fewer days with parents than I had been doing in the summer. This was a bold step for me. We were at peace with our calendar, and I asked Dan to please remind me to stay true to it, even when opposition would arise.

Help came from mom. My mom is a saint– really! She felt called to gather her daughters together for prayer before creating a new schedule. After we prayed, she said one of the most profound things I have ever heard… profound in its simplicity: "God honors decisions made in love." As our family seeks to be present for dad, everything we do must be with great love. This is how there will be peace in our home. Mom grounded me in love.

Help came in reading and meditation of Scripture, asking God to show me the way. One gospel story that spoke volumes to me was the parable of the Wise and Foolish Virgins (Mt 25:1-13). The wise virgins were prepared with extra oil in their flasks. The foolish ones were not. Part of preparing for dad's transition to new life is having adequate systems and people in place to give the proper extra care when needed. In addition to hospice care, we need back up help to help us! Finding outside resources to help our family navigate end of life will allow all of us to be fully present as our truest selves and flourish in peace as a unified family.

Help came in the presence of a priceless friend, Deb. After a challenging family meeting about the fall schedule, where expectations about unrealistic time commitments came up, I went for a walk to clear my head and called her. The brilliant coach she is, Deb asked me the right questions to help me remember my calendar decision. That decision had been with love and in union with my husband. She congratulated me on staying true to myself and acknowledged that this is a growth edge for me. Deb reminded me to stay true to me.

Help came in dialogue with two mastermind communities I belong to. It is a blessing to be in the presence of powerful, compassionate, wise women who seek to make this world a better place. Our collective wisdom opened up stories shared by those who have gone on this journey before me as they tapped into their lived experiences to help me navigate my own. Heart attack, migraine headaches, anxiety, weight loss, mini strokes, gastrointestinal issues were some the results of long-term immersion in stressful life situations, and I couldn't help but think to myself ,"That's going to be me really soon if something doesn't change! Then I will be no good to anyone!" I needed to hear their truth to help me find my truth.

Marci Shimoff made a profound statement that rings so true to me in this moment, and it goes something like this: when your "no" is a soul "no," and you honor it, others eventually will be blessed and benefit by it. That makes total sense to me right now because by limiting my availability over the fall season, this "no" is actually opening the door to allow outside help to come in.

Building upon all this wisdom and help, and tapping into a reconnection with myself, it is clear my heart's longing is to be a daughter, not a professional caregiver experienced working with the dying. All summer, I tried to function as both. As time goes on, mom and dad will need me as their daughter, not the one getting up four times a night to help dad. They will need me to be their confidant, their companion, their processor, their eyes and ears, their competent and yet little girl who loves them very much. Without self-care, I am present in these roles as a shadow of who I am when I have restorative rest and show up fully present.

I am making the choice now to give from a cup that is overflowing and spilling into and out of the saucer. No more giving from a cup less than half full.

With this loving, courageous stance, I proclaim the following truths to stand on, even as I continue to figure out this new way of being in the world:

Stay deeply connected with my husband and be fully present when we are together. Keep my marriage at the center of all decision-making, especially when I want to give in and give up just to please others. This keeps me grounded and offers stability in an ever-changing reality.

Honor my conviction to show up for my parents as their loving and strong daughter offering them some of my greatest gifts: companionship; communal prayer together as we watch the daily Catholic TV mass and hold hands during the Our Father and offer hugs and kisses during the sign of peace; financial and business help; sharing memories through music, stories, and photos; and being a good listener allowing my parents to say what they need to say and allowing it to be heard without judgment. I love my parents so much that I am willing to make the sacrifice to put my self-care first. In this way, they will be able to receive all of me instead of part of me.

Stay connected to the incredible people God has blessed me with who generously share their stories, their wisdom, their love as a means of support to let me know we are on this journey together and it will all be ok. They are there for me, even when I am unable to reach out to ask for help and keep me grounded so I can take the next step.

Strive to be an advocate for each family member. By seeking to put myself in their shoes, I can release judgment and pain as we try to figure things out. This helps me let them be them and me be me. We are all doing the best we can with what we have.

Remember to remember who I am and why I am here on this earth at this time: to be a global missioner and remind others that God loves them very much. This is the core of my life vocation and God is challenging me to share this with my own family now, which is a humbling experience.

As I look to the future, it will continue to take courage to both stand up for Tina and stand in solidarity with Dan, dad, mom, and my family. This journey we are on is the road to holiness. Under the umbrella of God's unconditional love there are joys, trials, sufferings, laughs, letting go, and, in that right time, surrender. It will not always be easy. It will require me to pull up my big girl panties, own the size of myself, and continue to trust God will lead the way as long as I stay receptive to love– love for God, love for others, love for self.

TINA M MOREAU-JONES

After 40 years of experience in education, intercultural ministry and entrepreneurship, Tina Moreau-Jones is now looking through the lens of her legacy, to inspire others to create value and honor their own living legacy. Leading retreats, workshops and participating in Theological Reflection Groups has given her the opportunity to join our collective legacies with inspired intention.

Bridging the gap between inner beauty and outer beauty in the traditional direct sales industry, Tina is building teams of authentic women to embrace the fullness and power of their femininity, offering opportunities for women to recognize their inner beauty as the gateway to their soul. She inspires women to embrace courage and integrate their life experiences to access the fullness of what their calling is to be, to do, and to have in and for our world.

Connect with Tina at https://www.beherenowdt.com.

Embracing Courage with Faith

Yared Afework Demeke

As a child growing up in Ethiopia, I faced many challenges that required me to learn to be courageous. I survived war, famine, smallpox, and the ongoing struggles of living in an impoverished country. During the chaos of the Somalian invasion of Ethiopia, I became separated from my family and I remember sitting alone beside dead bodies while I tried to find my parents. As a young adult, I worked hard to earn a spot at university and build a successful career. I left my homeland and moved with my wife and baby daughter to Dubai, Greece, Italy, and then settled in Canada. All of these events in my life took enormous courage to navigate, but the time in life that I feel tested the limits of my courage, tenacity, and resilience came when I thought my struggles were over. Life threw a twist at me that I wasn't expecting.

After giving 15 years of dedication and demonstrated accomplishment with one employer, I was blindsided when my supervisor walked up to my desk and told me I was being let go from my job immediately. No reason was given, no opportunity for discussion. She ordered me to hand over my company phone, laptop, and keys to my company car. I was quickly walked out of the office and sent home in a taxi. I was not allowed to say goodbye to my long-time co-workers, and I was ordered to have no contact with them. To this day, I have received no explanation for this abrupt end to my job and my career.

As you might imagine, I was in shock. At first I thought it was a joke, some kind of sick prank. It made no sense. My work reviews had always been excellent and there had been no suggestion of any issues with my work or me personally. Since I had worked for this company for so long, I did not have my own cell phone or my own car. Having these pulled away from me I was left with no contacts and no way to get around with my young family.

The shock of this event also hit my wife and our two daughters. My friends and community could not believe I had been treated in such a disrespectful way with no explanation. How could I explain something to others that I couldn't even explain to myself? It made no sense at all.

As the disbelief faded into the realization that I had to start from scratch and reinvent my career, I started my journey of building a new life. I had moved around the world with that employer and created my life in Canada in that position, so I had never had to look for work in Canada before. Now I needed to figure out how to market my skills and learn how to apply for new jobs. Potential employers were not very supportive when I couldn't explain the gap in my employment. As the only source of income for my young family, I had no choice but to take on any work that I could find just to pay the bills and put food on the table.

My saving grace was my faith in myself and the universe. I had always been keen to learn lessons from thought leaders around the world. I believed that I could figure this out and create a new life for my family. I also knew it would be a tough challenge. I did everything I could to hold onto a positive mindset and take one step at a time, even when I was uncertain about where the steps were taking me. I did not allow myself to dwell on anger and resentment toward the employer who had treated me so poorly. I knew that emotions like that would only drain my energy and waste my time. I needed to focus on my goals for the future, not dwell on the pain of the past.

As I set out on this journey to recreate a life that allowed me to look after my family and be of service to the world, I learned several lessons along the way that supported me as I embraced the courage to create my own path. I am sharing these lessons with you in hopes that they will add value to you as you embark on new journeys.

Working hard doesn't always get you where you need to be.

In my younger years I believed if I was dedicated and worked hard for an employer, they would return the loyalty and respect. I dedicated 15 years of my life, working overtime and extra days without extra pay. I gave my time to my employer rather than spending more precious time with my young family. After being walked out the door from my job and treated with no respect or compassion, I realized that my belief was misguided. I will never get back that time I lost with family, but I will also never again allow someone else to set my priorities in life.

Most challenges come with a painful transition.

One of the biggest challenges of my journey in reinventing my life came as I struggled through the pain of leaving behind everything I had known in my life in order to start a whole new chapter. I had not anticipated the stress, overwhelm and heartbreak that comes with moving my life in a direction that my community did not understand. I hadn't expected the pain that came with leaving behind friends and co-workers who had been an important part of my past life. This painful transition was necessary for me to find the courage to leave behind my past career and start my own business, learn a new industry and new ways of doing business. I had to embrace courage to create a life that is fulfilling and of service.

Apply tenacity and keep moving forward.

As I came to the realization that not everyone around me would always understand or support my new vision, I also had to come to the realization that this journey was one that I would need to carry on my own shoulders. I needed to keep moving forward with my goals no matter how others might react. I needed to take on the challenges and remain tenacious to reach my new goals. Resilience and tenacity are required to find your own way when others don't believe in your vision.

Take on the mindset of Zero (0) Expectations.

In order to keep myself focused, I needed to take on the mindset of zero expectations from others. I had to start from the point of expecting nothing from them. This way I would not be disappointed if they were unsupportive, and I would be pleasantly surprised when they did give me encouragement. You need to trust yourself and find your way. Don't take on anger and resentment toward the people who have disrespected and hurt you.

Final Rewards are found after following your own passion.

After months of facing the challenges of finding my new path, I finally started to see my new life unfolding in front of me. The fog gradually cleared, and I could see that my hard work had started to pay off. Although I had needed to shift some aspects of my community as I evolved, I have created a whole new circle of friends who are supportive and encouraging.

I also developed some strategies and habits that allowed me to remain focused, positive, and always adapting.

I love to read the works of thought leaders from around the world. Their words of wisdom and perspective on personal growth help me to expand my vision of what is possible for me. Never underestimate the impact of the lessons learned from life experience and reading. What we absorb throughout life comes back to us when we need it.

Here are some of the books that I find very helpful in personal development and business:

1. *Think and Grow Rich* by Napoleon Hill
2. *The Ultimate Sales Machine* by Chet Holmes

3. *The EOS Life* by Gino Wickman
4. *Get a Grip by* Gino Wickman
5. *The E-Myth Revised* by Michael E. Gerber
6. *The Gain and the Gap* by Dan Sullivan

Another strategy I use to help me get clear on my vision and to embrace the courage to take on the challenges despite the fear and uncertainty involves journaling. For big decisions, I write out my choices and 'worst case scenarios.' I allow myself to consider all of the things that could go wrong, then write them down. I make the decision to move forward despite these issues if … I sometimes go back to review my decisions and remind myself of the factors I considered. Make the decision and move forward immediately.

We will all face major challenges at some point in our lives. We will come up against obstacles that seem insurmountable. We will be hit by events that seem to knock us backwards or completely off track from the path we were on. These are the times that we must summon up our resilience and tenacity to embrace courage. It is courage and our faith in ourselves that will help us to adapt and evolve in ways that create a new path.

Don't allow yourself to feel alone in your journey. Remember, we are all connected through a universal source. God is my guide and source of my life. You may call it by different names, but we all have this common connection that binds us. We all have a purpose and a contribution to make while we are here on earth. Even if some members of your community do not understand and share your mission, reach out and connect with other people who do. Surround yourself with people who will support and encourage you. Find strategies and habits that allow you to embrace courage and reach your big dreams.

As an immigrant to Canada, I have discovered a large gap in the system that can make it very challenging for newcomers to navigate the systems and create a fulfilling, sustainable living. Part of my goal is to close this gap and build new levels of communication and connections between the support available and the people who need it.

My vision for my life's work, and the purpose for sharing my story here, is to inspire others to be courageous in their approach to life. Don't allow yourself to be held back by fear and overwhelm. Create your vision and step into it with courage.

Many people ask how they will know what their purpose in life is? My advice is to listen to your intuition. Pay attention to what feels right. I find these feelings of knowing come to me through prayer and connection with nature. By sitting quietly, looking out at the ocean, and asking God what his intentions are for me, I experience ideas and intuitive thoughts to follow a certain path. Don't let yourself get bogged down worrying about HOW you will accomplish your goal. Stay focused on the next step and trust you will find a way. You will find that resources will come to you as you make decisions that lead you in the direction of your calling. Allow yourself to pay attention to the impulses that come to you. Pay attention to the feelings you get in your soul and gut when you are considering new ideas. Trust your intuition and follow your heart.

When your purpose is focused on supporting people, nature, and the universe, you will find the way to reach your goals. Reach out and connect with communities of people who reinforce your positive mindset and encourage you to move forward with your goals. Embrace courage and take the next best step toward your vision and your dreams. We each have the capacity to accomplish amazing things. Have faith in yourself and God to create the way. Remember, we are all connected to each other and the nature through God and a universal energy.

YARED AFEWORK DEMEKE

Yared Afework Demeke lives in three continents (born in Harar, Ethiopia, Africa continent; lives and works in Dubai, Middle East, Asia continent; and for the last 15 years he has lived and worked in Vancouver, Canada, North America continent). He has faced many challenges and has discovered how to turn his challenges into opportunities.

Yared's professional journey starts as a teacher in technical institutes after graduating from Kotobe Metropolitan University (KMPU) to study electrical engineering at Adama Science and Technology University (ASTU) to Project Management (PMI) and, finally, awarded Master residential builder at Canada (HAVEN). Yared has international certifications on Passive house trades person from Passive house institute (PHI).

He has gone from being in a refugee camp to now owning five companies in Canada. His businesses include construction, elevator, manufacturing, and coffee. He lives in Vancouver, Canada, with his beautiful wife, Bety, and his two kind daughters, Kine and Hessed. Yared is a lifetime student and he is still taking courses.

Yared has taken interest in personal development and loves sharing his wisdom with others in order to help them become their own best version of themselves. His faith in GOD and himself has allowed him to overcome many challenges. He is currently working on his own book, which he will share his experiences and lessons with the world.

Connect with Yared at Yared.a@alairhomes.com.

CPSIA information can be obtained
at www.ICGtesting.com
Printed in the USA
BVHW040733141222
654183BV00001B/62